The Chair

In his notes, the author says, "I think that The Chair is a good story. I hope that The Chair is nothing more than a good story." You must judge for yourselves. One thing is certain –a simple plot is turned into a series of events that will challenge your mind and question your basic beliefs.

You will find yourself discussing this book with family and friends. You may find yourself agonizing over the questions that it poses. But, only when your final curtain falls will you know for sure if the Chair was just 'a good story.'

The Chair

by
Eric Pullin

Published by
Inknbeans Press

Cover: Leigh Young

My special thanks to Jo and to Susan at Inknbeans Press.

Thank you, Jo, for your never-ending support and encouragement and for your infectious enthusiasm.

Thank you Susan, (my editor), whose amazing talent has turned my abomination of the English language into a readable and, I hope, enjoyable passage of text.

I feel that this is your book as much as it is mine.

Author's Note

Are you awake?
Are you sure that you are awake?
Can you prove that you are awake?
Think very carefully about that last question.
Dreams are the reality of the subconscious mind. It is only
when you wake that you become aware that you were
dreaming.

But what if waking from a nightmare was all a part of that
nightmare? What if waking up this morning was all part of your
dream?
What if you're really still asleep?

So I'll ask you again.
Are you awake?
Can you prove that you are awake?
I don't believe that you can!

Enjoy "The Chair"
I hope that the story makes you think.
Writing it has certainly made me think.

Eric Pullin

Prologue

She had been asleep on the living room couch. The musical chime of the front door bell had woken her. A glance at her watch told her it was nearly 1.30am. Who the hell could be ringing at this hour of the night? Had Paul forgotten his keys again? Semi-conscious, she stumbled out of the room and into the dark hallway towards the front door.

She placed a bleary eye against the spy-hole. What she saw in the small circular frame jerked her whole body into action and her mind into overdrive. For an instant, she froze and then nervously opened the door.

"Mrs Ford?" the young policewoman enquired.

Jo nodded.

"May we come in, Mrs Ford?"

With her mind racing, Jo opened the door to allow the policewoman and her male companion into the hallway.

"What's happened?" she asked, hardly wanting to hear an answer.

"Maybe we could go and sit down somewhere," the male police officer said. At that instant, Jo knew that her whole life was about to change.

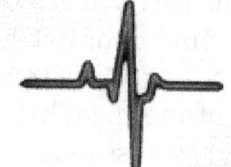

Chapter 1

"There's been a road accident involving your husband Paul." It was the policeman's voice with words that she would never forget.

Her stomach tightened; her lips moved, but the obvious question would not come out.

The policewoman, who sat next to her on the couch, took her hand and squeezed gently.

After a short pause to allow the initial information to sink in, the policeman continued. "Paul has been taken to hospital in Wolverhampton. We don't have any details. All we know is that he is alive and being looked after. We can take you to him."

"He's going to be okay?" Jo managed in a voice that pleaded for a positive response. Regaining some composure, she said, "How stupid of me. I know that you can't answer that question. What happened? Where did it happen? When did it happen? He called me at around 9pm. He was on his way home from Scotland."

"Why don't we ask Sally to make a pot of tea?" the policeman said, looking towards his partner. "A hot drink will do you good and it will give you a few minutes think. There will be plenty of time to talk about what's happened. Right now, just concentrate on the fact that Paul is in the very best hands and the best thing you can do is go to him."

"Of course." Jo said, "I'll get a few things together to take to the hospital."

Sally had already moved towards the kitchen to make tea as Jo climbed the stairs.

Once in the bedroom, Jo finally felt the tears streaming down her cheeks. She sat, head in hands, on the corner of their bed. Bleak images of horrendous injuries flashed through her mind. "Stop!" she told herself. "He's alive – he's going to be fine. Just pull yourself together, for God's sake!"

A tap on the bedroom door and Sally saying, "Tea's made," brought Jo back to her senses.

The journey to the Royal Hospital in Wolverhampton was quiet. Jo sat in the back of the police car trying to stop herself from thinking too much about what might have happened to her husband.

They had been married for six years – a holiday romance that had blossomed into a blissfully happy relationship. Jo was a teacher; Paul was a budding actor who could turn his hand to just about anything to earn a living between parts.

His trip to Scotland had been to audition for a minor role in a new stage play. Paul had been certain – as always – that this was the role that would lead to bigger and better parts. Jo – as always – supported him fully, knowing that, for him to be happy, he needed the footlights and the applause.

The only cloud in their marriage had been the lack of a child. No medical reasons accounted for the fact that five years of trying had proved fruitless. Over the last twelve months, they had both seemed to accept they would remain childless; the subject was no longer discussed. Her tears began to flow again as Jo considered that being childless might now be a blessing in disguise.

The police car stopped outside the hospital's Accident and Emergency entrance and Sally took Jo inside. Sally spoke to the woman at the reception desk and, after a brief conversation, she led Jo through some swing doors where they were met by a uniformed nurse. Sally took Jo's hand again and tried to smile as she wished her good luck and said her goodbyes. Jo had the feeling that Sally knew far more than she was telling but she thanked her for her kindness and turned to follow the nurse along the cream-and-blue-painted corridor. The squeak of their shoes on the plastic floor tiles gave an eerie echo in the silence.

Halfway along the corridor, the nurse stopped and opened a door. Jo followed her into a small room with a low coffee table strewn with magazines and four upholstered chairs.

"Sit yourself down, love," the nurse said. "I'll find you a nice cup of tea and a doctor will be along to talk to you in a few minutes."

She turned to leave the room.

"Wait! You must be able to tell me something about my husband – something to prepare me for what the doctor is going to say."

"Don't you fret, love," the nurse replied. "All I know is that your husband will be getting the very best care and attention that's possible. I haven't been involved with his case, so I really don't know anything. But I do know he couldn't be in better hands. I promise you won't be kept waiting for too long. I'll pop back with a hot drink. Just try to be calm."

With that, the door closed and Jo was left alone with her thoughts. She picked up a magazine and immediately put it down again. She suddenly remembered she had left the small case that she had packed with toiletries for Paul in the back of the police car. She searched her handbag for a mirror to see how she looked and was shocked by the sight. As she replaced the mirror in her bag, she noticed her spare set of keys to the Audi Coupe – Paul's pride and joy. It was a gift from his parents, who were wonderfully, filthy rich. "Bloody car!" she thought. "He always drives too fast if I'm not with him."

The nurse returned with a plastic cup of warmish tea. As soon as she entered the room, her demeanour raised Jo's hopes.

"I've made a few enquiries," she said. "Don't you go telling the doctors that I've been poking my nose in, but, from what I can gather, your husband is stable. He is pretty poorly, but you can stop fearing the worst. I'd better not say any more or I'll find myself in trouble. Now drink your tea – the doctor's on his way."

Jo looked at the grey-haired nurse and managed to raise a weak smile. "Thank you!" she said. "Thank you for caring."

Jo found herself standing up as the dark-suited man entered the room. He held his hand out for Jo to shake as he said, "I'm Doctor Portman. I'm the consultant looking after Paul. Please sit down, Mrs Ford."

"It's Jo. Do call me Jo. Please tell me what's happened to Paul."

Jo felt a sudden blush of shame as she registered that Dr Portman was an extremely good-looking man.

"As I'm sure you know from the police, Paul has been involved in a road accident. Let me say, first of all, that his present condition is serious but stable. He has suffered a number of injuries. He has two broken legs – which will mend, of course. He has certain internal injuries that are causing us some concern. We will be operating on Paul in the next few hours. We will know more once the operation is complete, but these injuries are not considered to be life threatening.

"Our main concern is that Paul sustained fairly serious head injuries; we are monitoring his condition very closely. As always, in these situations, we have to fix whatever we know we can fix first and then see where we stand.

"The operation tonight will be to assess and repair his internal injuries, and we'll also look after the broken bones. I don't see any major problems with this part of Paul's treatment.

"As for the head trauma, it's very difficult to make a detailed assessment until we have been able to carry out a number of tests. At the moment, Paul is not conscious. That is probably a very good thing for Paul, but makes our job more difficult.

"The best summary I can offer at this stage is that your husband is very ill and is going to need fairly lengthy medical attention. However, I can see no reason – unless we encounter the unexpected – why he cannot make a full *physical* recovery. However, it will be a while before any of us know how serious - or not - any damage to his brain may be.

"I understand how great a shock all of this must be to you. All I can promise you, Jo, is that we will give Paul the very best care. At this stage, you should be optimistic that we will be able to return your husband to you fit and well – though it's going to take some time." Dr. Portman waited whilst Jo absorbed the information he had given to her.

After a lengthy silence, Jo began to sob.

The doctor reached over and took her hand.

"I'm sorry, Dr. Portman," Jo whispered. "It's all a bit much to try to take in. Can I see Paul? Is there anything at all I can do?"

"Of course you can see him – but, as I said, he's not conscious at the moment. I must warn you that he looks in a bit of a state, but we'll fix all that. You must try not to be too upset when you see him. There's little you can do for him right now. You must trust in the team that's looking after him. Your job will start when he regains consciousness. Paul is going to need a lot of love and support over the coming days and weeks – even months.

"I do need you to sign some consent forms as Paul's next of kin so that we can start the treatment he needs. I'll ask a nurse to bring those to you. She will also arrange for you to see him before he goes for surgery.

"Listen to me, Jo - Paul is very lucky to be alive from what the police have told me. But he *is* alive and right now he has every chance of recovery. There is a room that you can stay in at the hospital if you like, but I suggest that you would be better going home or going to stay with friends or family – certainly for tonight, at least.

"I'm going to give you my personal telephone number here at the hospital. You can call anytime – day or night – and either I or one of the team will talk to you. What has happened can't be changed, Jo. All we can do now is to work together for Paul's future. Be strong. Paul is going to need you to be strong."

Dr Portman stood and offered his hand to Jo again. She shook it as she thanked him for his frankness. The doctor felt in his pocket and handed Jo a business card. "Use this number anytime," he repeated. "I must go and prepare to look after Paul. A nurse will be along in a few minutes to take you to see him."

As he turned to leave the room he stopped and reached back to touch Jo's arm. With the warmest of smiles and in the softest voice, he said, "Have faith, Jo. Trust me – I'm a doctor."

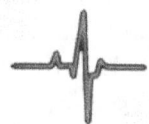

Chapter 2

About ten minutes passed before a young, dark-skinned nurse entered the room carrying a brown folder.

"Hello Jo, I'm Kathy. I'm on Doctor Portman's team, so I'll be looking after Paul." Kathy offered her hand for Jo to shake. "How are you feeling?" The look on Jo's face made the young nurse add, "Sorry – stupid question."

"No – it's okay," Jo said. "I'm fine – just trying to let everything sink in. I'm fine, really."

"I hate to sound so practical at a time like this," Kathy said, "but there are a couple of papers we need you to sign. We have to get Paul prepped for surgery."

She opened the folder on the coffee table and handed Jo two sheets of paper and a ballpoint.

"Just a squiggle at the bottom of each page and then we can get on with what needs to be done. I'll be with him all the way, and I promise to call you as soon as we are out of surgery. Try not to worry too much. Doctor Portman's fantastic. Paul couldn't be in better hands."

Jo signed without bothering to read and handed the papers back to Kathy.

"Now, I'm sure you would like to see Paul before we—"

Jo stopped her in mid-sentence. "I think I've changed my mind. Of course I want to see him, but Doctor Portman warned me that he was in a bit of a state, and all I really want to see is *my* Paul. If he's still unconscious, I don't think that seeing him now will do either of us any good. It's best that you just do whatever has to be done as quickly as possible without me getting in the way. I do hope you understand."

"Of course," Kathy said, reaching to give Jo's hand a squeeze. "Why don't you pop off home and try to get some rest. It's going to be several hours before Paul's out of the theatre. I'll call you and let you know that everything's okay. Get some sleep.

You're going to need it. You have a tough time in front of you, but we're all here to help."

Jo managed a weak smile and said, "Thank you," as Kathy left the room. She sat for several minutes just trying to come to terms with the events of the past couple of hours.

It was after 4.30am when the taxi dropped Jo at her home. Her mind was still in a daze and her imagination was still racing. She should have gone to see Paul. What if something went wrong on the operating table? What if she never had the chance to see him again? "Stupid! Stupid bitch!" she said to herself. "Why didn't you think before saying no?"

The tears began again as Jo climbed the stairs and collapsed onto her bed. She realised this was the first time she had been truly alone since the police knocked at her door and broke the terrible news. Jo sobbed uncontrollably.

Jo was awakened by the bedside telephone's silly ring tone. It took her a moment to remember what had happened – but only a moment. She answered the phone.

"Hello Jo. It's Kathy at the hospital. Just wanted to let you know that Paul is fine after surgery. Everything went to plan – in fact, things weren't as bad as we had first imagined. He's all patched up now and looking so much better. He hasn't woken up yet, so there's no rush for you to get here. But do come along when you're ready to."

"Oh, that's wonderful to hear. Thank you so much, Kathy. I'll be along as soon as I'm up."

"You just take your time, Jo. Have something to eat and drink. The food here is pretty average, so best get something before you come. If there's any further news, I'll call you. Paul's just sleeping peacefully and the longer he can sleep, the better. We're keeping a constant eye on him, so try not to worry."

"Bless you!" Jo said and ended the call.

She glanced at her watch – it was 8.50am. Saturday – thank God. No school to be late for. After showering and dressing, she managed a piece of toast with her coffee. It suddenly dawned on her that there were things that she must do, people she needed to contact. What about Paul's parents? They didn't even know their son was lying in a hospital bed. What about the car? Where was it? As if she really cared!

As she was making a mental list, the front doorbell rang.

Jo opened the door to find Sally, who was holding the case that Jo had left in the back of the police car. "Hello, Jo. I was on my way home and I thought I'd better let you have this back. Just finished my shift. I only live just round the corner in Wyndham Road – number 17 – so no trouble just to pop this in to you. How's Paul?"

"Sorry. Stupid of me to forget the case. The hospital has just been on the phone. They operated last night and all went well. He's in a pretty bad way, but so far, so good. Would you like to come in for a coffee or something? I could use the company."

"Maybe just for a few minutes – and a coffee sounds good."

Sally left her hat and coat on the hall stand and followed Jo into the kitchen.

"I was just thinking of all the things that needed to be done," Jo said. "You know – informing relatives and friends. I haven't even told his parents yet. They will be devastated. I'll have to get some time off work too, and then there's the car to sort out – insurance and all that."

"Everyone will rally round," Sally answered. "You'll be surprised how much help and support people will offer. You must take advantage of all the help that you can get. For the time being, forget the bloody car and ignore the bloody police and the insurance company. You have enough on your plate without worrying about things that will wait."

For the first time in what seemed an age, Jo smiled. "Ignore the bloody police? I'm sure your bosses would love to hear you saying that!"

Sally laughed. "They'll want interviews and information. They'll have paperwork to complete but, seriously, it can wait. You concentrate on the important things: looking after yourself and Paul."

"Do you enjoy your police work?" Jo asked.

"Love it!" Sally replied with a sparkle in her eyes. "It's all I can ever remember wanting to be. Dad was a copper. I guess it's in the blood. There *are* downsides, like last night – knocking on your door at 1.30 in the morning with bad news. That's tough to handle. They tell us that we should try to not become personally involved, but that's almost impossible. Of course it becomes personal. I'd have to be a pretty hard cow not to have any feelings for you and Paul."

"Thank you!" Jo said with tears in her eyes again, "I'll never swear at a traffic cop again – promise! Really, it must be difficult being the bearer of bad news. When you see the police at your door, they're hardly likely to be there to tell you you've won the lottery."

"Don't get me wrong: I really do love the job. There's plenty to compensate for the difficult bits. Listen, when Paul is well, we must all go out for a meal together and look back and laugh at all the tears and worrying. I'm going to leave you my phone number. You know where I live – number 17 Wyndham – just round the corner. If there is anything I can do, call me, any time day or night. If you need a bit of company, just shout. You can bet that I'll be calling you to find out how Paul is getting on." Sally stood up. "I really must go and get my beauty sleep. You hang tough and promise me that you'll keep in touch."

Jo put her arms around Sally and gave her a hug. "You must be the silver lining around my cloud," she said. "I promise I'll keep you informed and I promise that you're the one member of the bloody police that I won't ignore. Say thanks to your partner of last night from me. You were both so kind."

When Sally left, Jo picked up the phone to call her in-laws. Her own parents had died when she was still young, both victims of a boating accident. With no other immediate family to care for her, Jo had been fostered. But even her foster parents were gone now.

Mitchell and Grace, Paul's parents, had been Dad and Mum to her even before she had married Paul. They welcomed her into the family in such a way that it would have been impossible for Paul not to marry her. She loved them dearly. She had no idea how she was going to break the news to them.

Thankfully, it was Mitch who answered the phone.

"Hi, Dad."

"Hi, honey. To what do we owe a call at 9.30 on a Saturday morning? I thought you'd still be in bed!"

"Bad news Dad. There's no easy way to tell you. Paul's in hospital. He crashed the car on his way home last night." She waited.

"How bad?" Jo could hear the tremble in Mitch's voice.

"I wish I knew." Jo tried to hold back the sobs. "He underwent surgery last night for some broken bones and internal injuries. He's come through that okay, but the doctors are mainly concerned with his head injuries; they won't know how bad things are until they've run more tests." Once again, Jo waited.

When Mitch spoke, Jo could instantly tell that he had regained his composure. And his words touched her heart.

"Okay. Paul is in good hands. What about you, love? Who's looking after you?"

"Oh, Dad!" she cried. "I'm in pieces."

"Listen, honey. Mum and I are on our way. Don't try to say any more right now. We need to be together to talk this through. Just try to be calm. We'll be there as quickly as we can. We love you."

Jo could hear that even Mitch was having trouble now controlling his emotions. Though there was so much more to say, she simply said, "Bye, Dad – see you soon," and replaced the receiver.

It would take Paul's parents at least an hour to drive over. Jo tried to busy herself with household chores to pass the time. She would have plenty of time to pass alone in the house over the coming days.

After a while, she sat down at the kitchen table and started a list of people who would have to be informed of Paul's accident. Surprisingly, the list was quite short – just his agent and a couple of close friends. She was still racking her brain trying to ensure that she hadn't missed anybody out when the doorbell rang.

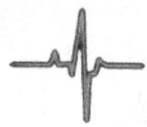

Chapter 3

The black Audi Coupe had torn through the roadside fencing and hit a tree. The impact had almost halved the vehicle lengthwise, and the mangled wreckage had come to rest half-cartwheeled, with its nose to the ground and its tail propped against a scarred tree trunk.

A full 80 metres away at the bottom of a steep embankment lay the overturned remains of the second Audi Coupe, its white bodywork streaked in mud and grass where it had rolled to a stop. The three wheels that remained attached to the car pointed skywards. The roof had totally collapsed. Every piece of glass had shattered.

The two policemen stood beside the once-white car and looked at the remains with amazement.

"How in hell's name did the driver come out of that alive?" one of them asked. "Look at it – it's as flat as a pancake! You couldn't squeeze a cat into the driver's seat, let alone a fully grown man!"

"Must have been some bloody show," the other said. "There must be nearly 100 metres between them, yet they came through the fencing at virtually the same point. Think of the speed at which they must have been travelling."

As they talked, they noticed a figure close to the black Audi.

"Who the hell is that? Hey you! Get away from that car. This is a police accident scene!" Turning to his companion, he said, "Come on. We'd better get up there fast before he starts nicking bits."

"Bet you a quid it's a reporter." the other one said.

The two men started running up the steep incline towards the figure. As they got nearer, the man moved out of sight behind the twisted wreck. When they reached the car, the man was nowhere to be seen.

"That's impossible! He can't just disappear into thin air. There's no way he could have moved away from the tree without us seeing him. You did see him, didn't you? I'm not imagining things, am I?"

"He was there, right enough, but God knows where he is now. Bloody Houdini. Either that or I need new glasses and you need an eye test!"

"Maybe it was the ghost of the driver," the first policeman said with a glint in his eye.

"Aye, right! And I suppose you're going to put that in your report, are you?

Come on. Let's get this place cordoned off and get back to the station - not that a bit of sticky tape is going to keep the vultures away."

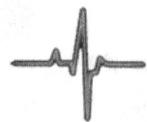

Chapter 4

When Jo opened the front door to Mitch and Grace, there were the inevitable tears. The three of them made their way to the kitchen. Jo put the kettle on and they sat around the small table.

The grief that she saw in the faces of Paul's parents somehow made her own feelings easier to bear. They were all suffering the same emotions and their sorrow was helping her – but not much.

Jo recounted the events of the last ten hours in as much detail as she could manage. Mitch and Grace listened intently, not wanting to interrupt.

When she finished, she waited for a long moment as they sat without speaking, each lost in their private thoughts.

It was Mitch who broke the silence. "Okay, honey, let's just have a think about where we are now. Paul is being well cared for. If we are needed, or if there is any news, the hospital will be straight onto us. There's nothing we can do for Paul right now except pray. We have to think about the practical things. There will be people who need to be informed—"

"I was making a list when you arrived," Jo butted in. She handed Mitch the piece of paper that she had been writing on. "I can't think of anybody else offhand."

"Good girl. I want you to leave this to me. There's no point in you upsetting yourself by describing what's happened over and over again. I'll speak to these people – if that's alright with you."

"Thanks Dad. I wasn't looking forward to talking to everyone right now. You'd better leave the school to me. I'll call them first thing on Monday and explain that I'm going to need some time."

"There will be things to do with the car and the insurance and probably the police too," Mitch continued. "You don't have to worry about any of that. I'll take care of it."

Jo told them about her visit from Sally and how she had already been told to "ignore the bloody police." The story raised a smile from her in-laws.

"What are your plans about going to the hospital?" Mitch asked.

"I'd like to go there now, if that's okay with both of you. I know that I won't be able to do anything useful, but I just feel that I should be close to him. I'm still cursing myself for not having the courage to see him before he went to theatre last night. I want to see him now."

"So do we," Grace said. "It will be easier if we are all together to support one another."

"I'd like to talk to his doctors too, if that's okay with you, honey. I don't want you to feel that I'm trying to take over or anything, but I'd like to hear what they have to say."

"Of course, Dad. He's your only son. Of course you want to be involved in everything – and you too, Mum. I want you to be involved. I need you to help me."

Mitch stood up. "Come on – group hug. We'll all come through this together. Paul's made of strong stuff, just like his Dad."

The three of them hugged and Mitch said a little prayer asking for Paul to be returned to them in perfect health.

"One more thing before we go," Mitch said, "and I won't take no for an answer. I'm going to transfer some money into your bank, Jo. And before you tell me—"

"It's okay, Dad...honestly. I'll ask if I need help."

"Listen to me Jo," Mitch pleaded. "Let me do this for my own peace of mind if nothing else. There are going to be expenses, like getting to and from the hospital: taxis or hire cars. I bet you won't feel much like cooking, so you'll be grabbing a 'take-away' or snatching a bite in town. There may be things you need to get for Paul. Look at the bigger picture. You need transport; we have to get you another car. You may need to get help to look after Paul when he comes home. You know that your Mum and I have got money coming out of our ears. We can't buy Paul's health back...otherwise you'd have him back today. What we can do is make sure that money is never a problem. So please, Jo, let me do this. Everything that your Mum and I have will be coming to you two eventually. Give me the peace of mind in knowing that you don't have to think about money. "

"You know that Paul will be furious when he finds out, don't you, Dad?"

"I'd love Paul to be furious with me right now," Mitch said. "Don't worry about what he will think; he'll have enough sense to realise that it was the right thing to do."

"Okay, Dad – and thank you both for being so thoughtful." Jo gave them both another hug.

"Right, that's settled then," Mitch said. "Let's get ourselves off to the hospital and see Paul."

Jo hated hospitals – the endless sitting around and waiting. It didn't seem to matter which hospital it was or why you were there, waiting was bound to be a major part of your visit.

When Jo introduced herself at the reception desk, she was surprised and slightly concerned when they were not ushered to the nearest row of plastic chairs to wait for attention as she had expected. Instead, not only were they directed to the unit where Paul was being treated, but they were also given a young nurse to show them the way.

As they approached the double doors to Intensive Care Unit 3, the left-hand door swung towards them and Kathy appeared, dressed in her outside coat.

"Hi, Jo," she said with a smile.

"Are you still here?" Jo gasped.

"That's the lot of us nurses," Kathy said. "I have managed to grab a couple of hours, but I'm off home now until 2 pm tomorrow. I'm glad you caught me, though."

"How's Paul?" Jo asked, forgetting to introduce Mitch and Grace to Kathy.

Kathy held the swing door to the unit open for the three of them to enter and followed them back inside.

"There's not been too much change since I spoke to you this morning. Paul's still sleeping – sensible boy – so we're just monitoring him until he wakes up and we can talk to him. Come on, I'll introduce you to Ellie. We sort of share the time looking after Paul. Ellie's lovely. She'll look after you and take you to see Paul. I'm sure she'll find the doctors to come and have a chat with you too."

As they entered the small waiting room, Jo realised that she had totally ignored Grace and Mitch. "Oh, I'm so sorry," she said, turning towards them. "Kathy, this is Paul's mum and dad, Grace and Mitch Ford. I guess you'll be seeing plenty of them too while Paul's in here."

The parents shook hands with Kathy, who offered them tea or coffee. Neither accepted. Mitch asked Kathy how long she'd been nursing and looked surprised to hear that she had been at the hospital for over twelve years.

"Sit yourselves down," Kathy said, "and I'll go and find Ellie to come and look after you. She's been here even longer than me," she added, giving Mitch a rather mischievous look.

When she had left the room, Mitch looked sheepishly at Jo and said, "I wasn't trying to question her competence. She just looks so young."

"It's alright, Dad. She's got a sense of humour – I could tell from the look she gave you. I'm sure she doesn't blame you for wanting to make sure that Paul has the very best care the hospital can offer."

Kathy returned with a middle-aged nurse with flaming red hair and red-rimmed glasses to match. "This is Ellie," Kathy said, and it was no surprise when Ellie said hello to them all in a broad Irish accent.

"Now you go and get yourself off home," Ellie said, looking at Kathy. "I'll look after these good people. Go on – you've had a busy night."

Kathy smiled and waved goodbye.

"Now, you'll be wanting to see Paul, I'll bet. Before I take you in, I'd better tell you that he's pretty well bandaged up, so you can't see too much of his face, and he's attached to all sorts of wonderful machines that are monitoring just about everything that's going on. Don't be alarmed. He's fast asleep and not in any pain. You won't get any response from him; it's probably best if you don't try to speak to him or touch him. Doctor Portman is very keen that Paul should wake up of his own free will without any outside stimulation. I know that you'll probably want to give him a cuddle and let him know that you're here, but it's best to do what the doctor says, if you will."

"Of course," Jo said. "We'll just stay for a couple of minutes. We won't get in your way."

The scene in Paul's room was just as Ellie had described.

Paul's head and face were almost totally covered by dressings. Tubes and wires were attached to numerous points on his body. The wall behind his bed was a mass of computer screens, each one monitoring and displaying information about diverse bodily and mental functions.

It was easy, even for the uninitiated, to see from the screens that Paul's heartbeat was regular. His breathing was the only movement that could be seen from his body.

The three onlookers all held hands as their eyes surveyed their beloved Paul. They stood like statues, rooted to the spot, transfixed by a scene that was, at best, overwhelmingly distressing and, at worst, unmistakeably horrifying.

Jo let go of Mitch's hand and raised her own hand to her mouth to hold back a sob. Mitch put his arm around her shoulders and gave her a squeeze.

"Come on," he whispered, "we can do no good for Paul in here. Let's leave him to the medical team to look after."

Shocked and emotional, the three of them left the room and returned to the small waiting area where Ellie joined them.

"It's an awful shock," she said, "but don't be upset by all the gadgets in there. It's perfectly normal and they are all making sure that we are alerted to the slightest change in Paul's condition."

She held up a small black box that looked like a tiny remote control. "You see this little darling? This will go off like the mother of all alarm clocks if anything changes with Paul. Trust us – we will only be seconds away from his side if he needs us, day and night. Now, how about that cuppa tea? I'm sure you could all do with one. I'll have one of the girls bring it in to you whilst I see if I can find Doctor Portman to come and have a word. How's that?"

"Thank you Ellie." Grace answered. "That would be wonderful. I think that we could all do with just a few minutes to pull ourselves together. A nice cup of tea will help."

The tea arrived at the same time as the white-coated Dr Portman. Instead of the more usual plastic beakers, it came in a china pot with matching cups and saucers, as well as a milk jug and sugar bowl. Jo wondered if the upgrade was for the benefit of the relatives or the surgeon. She assumed the latter.

It was early afternoon now, and Jo marvelled at the thought that this man – still on duty – had probably saved her husband's life less than twelve hours ago.

Doctor Portman introduced himself to Mitch and Grace and smiled a hello to Jo.

"Shall I pour?" Grace offered.

"I'm told that you've been in to see Paul," he started. "Bit of a shock, I expect, but you really mustn't worry about all the wires and tubes. Most of all, you should know that Paul isn't in any pain.

"Everything that we've done so far has gone according to plan. We're basically just monitoring and waiting for Paul to wake up. He is not under any form of sedation. He is free to wake whenever his body and mind are ready. Once he is awake and we can talk to him, we will get a much better idea of where we are. He has been seen by our top neurosurgeon, Mr. Grayson, who believes no surgical procedures need to be considered at the moment. Mr Grayson will continue to consult on Paul's case.

"Physically, Paul can, and probably will, make a complete recovery. There is a 'but,' and at this stage I think that I must make it clear that it's quite a big 'but.' Putting it as plainly as I can, Paul's brain is extremely swollen from the trauma. The brain is a very complicated piece of equipment, as I'm sure you are all aware. The medical profession still has much to learn about the workings of this vital organ; one thing we do know is that pressure on the brain is never a good thing.

"Sometimes, the slightest bump to the head can have devastating consequences. On the other hand, sometimes trauma such as Paul has experienced can be recovered from with no ill effects. That's how fluid the situation is at the moment. I'm sorry that I can't be more specific. It would be wrong of me even to 'best guess' how Paul's case will turn out.

"We must all be optimistic – there is no point in looking on the black side. So, that's where we stand. Is there anything you would like to ask? I'll do my best to answer any questions you may have."

"Do you have any idea how long it may be before Paul wakes up?" Mitch asked.

"Not really. It could be sometime today, but I would not be concerned if he slept for many more hours. It's important to try to let Paul's body and mind decide when the time is right. I know it's frustrating for us who are trying to care for him. We want him awake so that we can assess his condition more accurately, but I am willing to wait. Of course, if he sleeps for too long, we will have to consider stimulating him into consciousness. But let's just wait and see for a while."

Mitch just had one more question. "Is there anything at all we can do right now? Any specialist equipment or specialist advice that could be helpful? Please don't think that I'm trying to throw money at the situation, but I am a very rich man, Doctor Portman, and if there is anything that you or the hospital needs to treat my son, you just have to ask." Turning to his daughter-in-law, he added, "I'm sorry, Jo, but it had to be said. That's my son lying there and I will not allow financial restrictions to hinder his recovery."

Doctor Portman did not seem in the least shocked at Mitch's outburst. "I fully understand your feelings, Mr Ford, and please rest assured that I will keep what you have said in mind. But let me also assure you that the equipment we have here and the talent of our doctors cannot be bettered. If, at any time, I feel there may be a direction we need to consider that might require your funding, I will certainly let you know. We are all here to do the best that we can for Paul, and I promise you that I will not let finance stand in the way of his treatment."

"Thank you, Doctor Portman. That's all I wanted to hear."

"You are all very welcome to stay around, if you so wish," the doctor said, standing to leave, "but I suggest it would be wiser for you to go to the comforts of your homes to wait, because waiting is all that any of us can do at the moment. We will keep you fully informed of any changes to Paul's condition."

When the doctor had gone, the three sat in silence for a few moments.

"Let's go home," Jo finally said.

"How about we go find something to eat?" Mitch suggested, "You have to eat, love, even if you don't feel hungry. Come on, we'll find somewhere quiet and have a chat about where we go from here."

The Chair

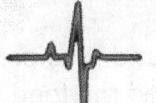

Chapter 5

The bistro they found was comfortable and quiet. They all commented on how good the food was, but no one could find the appetite to do it justice.

The conversation was subdued.

Mitch and Grace offered to spend a few days at Jo's. Jo thanked them but declined the offer, saying that she needed time and space. Mitch seemed to understand; Grace looked unconvinced.

They talked briefly about transport for Jo, but nothing was decided.

Mitch called for the bill and left a hefty tip on the table.

The drive back to Jo's was almost silent. When Mitch pulled up outside, it was accepted without discussion that Jo would go inside alone and Mitch and Grace would drive home.

Jo leaned forwards from the rear seat of the car and gave both Grace and Mitch kisses on their cheeks. "Thanks for being here with me. I'll call you often to let you know how things are. Love you, Mum. Love you, Dad."

And with that, she left them.

The clock above the fireplace said ten past five. Where had the day gone?

Loneliness soon kicked in. An empty house – an empty life without Paul. What *was* she going to do? She lay on the couch and closed her eyes. An age passed, yet when she looked at the clock again it said just five thirty.

She thought of Sally – just 'round the corner – and picked up the phone to call her. Sally's answer-phone told her to leave a message after the "beep." Jo didn't bother. She switched on the television and found an old black-and-white movie. Thankfully, it was so bad that it put her to sleep.

The telephone awakened her. Panic hit her: was it the hospital? Was it bad news? Trembling, she picked up the receiver.

"Hi, honey, it's Dad. Just to let you know that we got home safely and that I've put some funds into your bank. I want you to promise me that you'll hire a car for as long as Paul's in hospital. You have to be independently mobile. There should be plenty of money to see you through, but if you need more you only have to say. Now promise me!"

"Thank you, Dad. I promise that I'll fix up a hire car first thing in the morning."

"No more news from the hospital I suppose?" Mitch enquired.

"Nothing yet. In fact, when the phone rang, I half expected it to be them. You know I'll call you, Dad, as soon as I hear anything."

"I know you will, honey. It's just this damn waiting that's putting us all on edge. You try to get some sleep and we'll talk tomorrow."

"Night-night, Dad. I love you!"

"Night-night honey."

Jo decided on a hot bath and bed. She took the phone with her to the bathroom and started the taps running. As she undressed in her bedroom she had a strange feeling that someone was watching her. She spun round, not knowing what to expect.

A shadow seemed to pass across the mirror on the wardrobe door and then it was gone. She crossed her arms to cover her nakedness, but there was no need.

The deep, hot bath relaxed her. She lay there for over half an hour, just thinking. Her thoughts were more positive now than they had been since she first heard of Paul's accident.

She dried herself and pulled on a favourite old bathrobe. A glance at her watch told her that it was getting late. She considered trying Sally again, but not at this hour. Instead, she went downstairs to make herself a hot drink to take to bed.

As she filled the kettle, the front doorbell rang.

When she looked through the spy-hole in the front door she felt a terrifying sense of "deja-vu." Once again, in the circular frame, she saw a police uniform.

Her heart was pounding as she opened the door.

"Hi, Jo. Hope I haven't got you out of bed or anything."

"Oh, thank God, it's you, Sally!" Jo gasped as she opened the door wider. "Come in, come in."

"My, I have given you a fright, haven't I? I'm so sorry. We were just passing in the patrol car and I saw the lights on, Thought I'd pop in and see how things were going with Paul. I didn't think of the shock it might give you – ringing the bell at this time of night."

"It's okay, Sally. I'm just a bit on edge, I guess. Silly of me. Do come in. Don't stand out there."

"Well, just for a minute then. I've got my partner waiting in the car, so mustn't stay."

The two girls hugged as if they were lifelong friends.

"Not much news to give you, I'm afraid," Jo said. "Paul's mum and dad came over to the hospital with me today. They let us see him, but he's still sleeping and they asked us not to try to wake him. He's hooked up to so many machines! It looks awful." Tears welled again in her eyes.

"Hey, come on, Jo! They know what they're doing. Did they give you any idea of when he might come round?"

"He's been seen by a neurosurgeon who advised that he be allowed to sleep until his mind and body are ready to wake up naturally. Might be today...tomorrow...who knows. I just want to let him know that I'm there with him, helping him fight."

"It does sound sensible to let his mind decide when it wants to become active again," Sally said. "Listen, I'm off tomorrow. If you need a lift to the hospital, just give me a call. Tell you what, I'll give you a knock when I finish in the morning – should be about eight-ish. That's if you want me to, of course."

"Yes, please. I'll make us some breakfast and we can have a good chat. There's so much that I still don't know about what happened. Maybe you can fill me in."

"I'll try, but not if it's going to upset you. Look, I must go now...see you in the morning. Sleep tight." Sally was leaving when she suddenly turned and asked Jo, "Did you have another caller just before I arrived? I could have sworn that someone came out of your front gate as we pulled up, but when I got out of the car there wasn't a soul to be seen."

"No, no one's been here since I got home around five. How strange."

"He seemed like a youngish man - though I wasn't able to get a good look. Keep your doors locked, Jo. News travels fast, and there are people who are willing to take advantage of the kind of situation you're in. Not trying to spook you, but stay locked up, okay?"

"Thanks, Sally. I'll keep an eye out for anyone hanging around. Have a quiet shift."

"No chance," Sally laughed. "Sunday night is nutters night out round here. Night, Jo."

After Sally had gone, Jo remembered the shadow in the bedroom. Maybe somebody had been prowling around. There was a street light right outside that could have cast a shadow into the room.

She checked the locks on all the doors and windows and climbed the stairs to bed. As she lay there alone, the room felt cold and eerie. Jo shuddered and pulled the bedclothes tight around her neck. When sleep came, it was a deep and peaceful friend.

Chapter 6

She awoke with a start.

There was someone in the house; she could feel their presence. In the otherwise pitch–black room, the bedside clock glowed 4.38am.

Jo lay, rigid with fear, hardly daring to breathe. She listened: silence!

Several minutes passed – still nothing. She was beginning to relax when she heard it: not loud, but a definite crash, as if a glass had been dropped and broken.

Fear and panic gripped her. She looked for the phone and realised she had forgotten to bring the handset to bed with her. Her mobile? "Idiot! My bag's on the kitchen table!"

She threw back the sheets and grabbed her bathrobe from the bedside chair where she had discarded it. Through eyes that were slowly becoming accustomed to the darkness, she scanned the room for a weapon – anything. "God, Jo. Come on...think!" There was nothing.

Jo stood motionless, listening for – fearing – the sound of footsteps on the stairs. The second step from the top creaked. It always had done. She would know when the intruder was coming.

The only upstairs room with a lock on the door was the bathroom. The bedroom door was ajar. As silently as possible, Jo crept to the door. She could feel the beads of cold sweat forming on her face. Gently – oh, so gently – she opened the door a fraction more. She could see the top of the staircase that ran down into the hall. There was no sign of light or life. The bathroom was immediately to her left; no one could make it up the stairs before she could be safely locked behind its door. She waited, still listening for any giveaway noise that would let her know where the intruder was. The house was silent.

Glancing back at the bedside clock she saw 4.57am. "Twenty minutes...maybe they've gone." Jo made her mind up to get to the bathroom. The tiny window in there looked out from the side of the detached house. Even fully opened, it was too small to lean out of to call for help, but you could just see the street outside the front garden. Maybe she could attract attention if someone passed by. "Great plan, Jo!" she thought to herself. "Who's going to be walking along the road at 5am?" But the bathroom was still her safest bet. "Do I dash or do I creep?" Creeping won.

The bathroom door closed with a tiny "click." Jo held her breath and listened. Had the sound alerted the intruder that she was a wake and aware he or she was in the house? She turned the lock and sat on the floor with her back pressed against the door.

After a few minutes, Jo realised there was nothing more that she could do but to wait. There she stayed for what seemed like hours. Several times, she almost plucked up the courage to leave her hiding place but she always chickened out. She tried to convince herself that the intruder must have gone by now. But what if they hadn't?

Only when Jo noticed the first light of day through the frosted-glass window did she finally make up her mind to open the bathroom door.

She took the heaviest glass bottle she could find in the bathroom cabinet. At least it would be something she could throw if anyone came at her.

The sweat was back as she tiptoed down the staircase. The door of the kitchen was fully open; no one was in there. The living room door was open enough to see that there were no lights on.

Jo decided on a different tactic. She climbed the stairs again and stood outside the bathroom door, ready to lock herself in again. "Who's there?" she shouted as loudly as her trembling voice would allow. "I know you're down there – the police are on their way. I suggest you get out now!"

Nothing happened. Jo shouted again and waited. Still nothing.

A few minutes later, Jo had looked into all the downstairs rooms and checked all the locks on the doors and windows. Everything was secure. She was alone in the house.

She put the kettle on and made herself a pot of strong tea. She carried the steaming mug into the living room and slumped onto the couch. As her eyes scanned the room, she noticed something lying on the polished floor beside the drinks cabinet. It was one of the framed photographs that lived on top of that piece of furniture.

When Jo went to pick it up, she saw that it was the picture of Paul standing by his brand-new Audi Coupe, looking smug. The glass from the frame had smashed.

"That must have been the noise I heard," Jo said to herself. "What a bloody idiot! I've spent the night on the bathroom floor, terrified out of my wits, for nothing."

As she started to pick up the pieces of broken glass, Jo noticed a strange circular greyish stain on the floor. She rubbed at the edge of the stain with a wetted fingertip. It wouldn't budge.

She brought a cloth and floor polish from the kitchen and knelt down by the offending mark. Was she imagining things or was it getting fainter? She rubbed the edge of the stain again, this time with the cloth.

Slowly but surely, Jo watched the grey circle disappear before her very eyes. It took maybe five minutes for it to fade completely, but then it was gone, leaving not the slightest trace.

Jo, slightly perturbed, returned to her cooling mug of tea. The picture of Paul had sat happily atop the drinks cabinet for well over a year. Why fall down now? And that stain was definitely there. How could it just disappear?

As Jo pondered, the doorbell rang. It was Sally.

The Chair

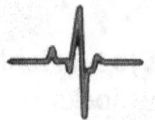

Chapter 7

The two traffic cops were back at the station. The accident scene had been cordoned off and investigated to the best of their ability. Measurements had been taken and notes made so that their reports could be submitted.

"Bloody paperwork! My life seems to revolve around bloody paperwork! Does anybody ever read this stuff? Do you think we should mention that bloke that we saw hanging around the black Audi, or just leave it out?"

"Better cover our tails and put it in, I guess," the second cop said. "What if the geezer pinched something that was lying around...something that turns out to be important? If we don't put him in the reports, someone might think we nicked it."

"How do you spell Houdini?"

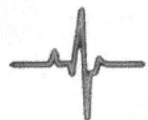

Chapter 8

As soon as Jo opened the door Sally asked, "You okay?"

"No news from the hospital," Jo replied. "Come on through, I'll put the kettle on."

"I bought a couple of bacon rolls from the all-night café on the corner. Hope you like bacon. It's always the same guy behind the counter. I don't know when he sleeps. Makes great bacon rolls, though."

"Bacon's fine, thanks," Jo said. "Sit yourself down. I'll grab a couple of plates."

"What's happened, Jo? You look shattered."

Sitting at the kitchen table, Jo recounted all of the night's events. Sally listened intently.

When Jo finished speaking, Sally got up and went to look at the back door. As well as the normal key lock, she saw a bolt near the top of the frame. The bolt was fully in place. Next she inspected the windows in the kitchen – all double-glazed with keys in place to lock the handles. "Are you fully double glazed?" she asked.

"Every window in the house – and I locked them all. I've checked them, too. They're still locked. I know what you're going to say: if everything's locked from the inside, nobody could have got in and out again. I've already reached that conclusion."

"Makes sense. Look, Jo, you're under immense pressure. I probably spooked you last night by saying that I thought I'd seen someone outside, and your mind did the rest. Pictures do fall down sometimes. Maybe one of Paul's parents took it down to look at when they were here and didn't put it back properly. The grey stain on the floor was probably just a shadow – a trick of light. You really shouldn't be all on your own at a time like this. Why don't you come and stay at my place, just for a few days? I've got a spare room. And if you didn't feel comfortable at any time, you could just pop back round the corner to your own house. What do you say? Let me be some company for you."

"And what are your bosses going to say about that?" Jo asked, "Remember what they teach you: no getting personally involved. I don't want to cause you any embarrassment."

"Stuff the bosses. How will they know anyhow? I'm off 'til Tuesday afternoon now. Give it a try. I can take you to the hospital – save you a taxi. And I'd like to see Paul too, if you don't mind. I'll feel so much better if you'll say yes."

"Let me think about it. It's so kind of you to offer but—"

She was cut short by the telephone ringing.

Sally watched as Jo answered the call. It was obvious from the conversation that it was the hospital on the other end of the line.

When Jo hung up, she looked worried.

"I have to meet with Doctor Portman at 11am. Paul's still sleeping. They wouldn't tell me anything else, but Portman wants to talk to me. I'm so scared, Sally!"

"Let me take you – you need someone to be with you. Try not to get all in a tizzy until you've heard what the doctor wants to say. Come on – come home with me now and I'll show you the room. It'll help you make your mind up if you want to stay for a few days, and it'll take your mind off things. I'll run you to the hospital in plenty of time for the meeting."

Jo didn't argue; a couple of minutes later, they were inside number 17 Wyndham Road.

When they arrived at the hospital at around 10.30am, Sally said she would go to the hospital café and wait for Jo there.

"No! Come to the meeting with me, Sal. I'll be able to cope so much better if you're there."

Sally could hardly refuse.

They were allowed to see Paul whilst they were waiting for Dr. Portman to arrive. The scene was exactly as Jo remembered. Ellie was still on duty. Kathy would be taking over at lunchtime.

A new nurse brought them coffee in plastic beakers. As 11am approached, they sat in virtual silence in the small waiting room.

Portman was late. When he finally arrived, he was accompanied by an older man in a grey suit, who turned out to be Dr Grayson.

The two doctors sat opposite Jo and Sally. Jo explained that Sally was a close friend with whom she would be staying for a few days. She added that Sally was not on duty – despite the police uniform. Sally smiled at the mention of her uniform and also with relief that Jo had decided to come and stay with her.

"As you know," Dr Portman said, "Paul is still sleeping – though he has tried to wake several times during the night. He hasn't been able to say anything to us yet. He has been conscious for only a couple of minutes at a time before falling back asleep. My concern is that our monitoring tells me that he quickly becomes very stressed mentally each time he wakes. Although increased mental activity is a good sign in the overall picture, stress of any kind is something he could well do without right now, whilst his body is trying to recover from its physical injuries.

"Because of my concerns, I asked Dr Grayson, our neurologist, to take another look at Paul and review all the data we have gathered. Doctor Grayson has offered a course of treatment that we want to discuss with you. I'll let Dr. Grayson explain."

Dr. Grayson spoke in a voice that immediately inspired confidence. "The first thing that I should say is that the signs are good. Every minute, our electronic gadgets feed us more information about Paul's condition. The brain is a funny piece of gear, but we can already tell there's plenty going on inside Paul's brain. That gives us good reason for hope. Once Paul wakes up properly, we will be able to test his responses accurately and we'll know, in greater detail, where we stand. David's – Dr

Portman's – concern is that if Paul wakes now, his mental state may hinder his recovery from his physical injuries. Up until now, we have allowed Paul to decide when he wakes and, as David has said, he has tried to wake several times without proper success. These failed attempts seem to have an adverse effect on his general condition. Both David and I are now of the opinion that we should take measures to ensure that we control his waking. We would like your consent to do what we feel is necessary."

Jo held her breath and squeezed Sally's hand.

"Please don't be alarmed at a term that I am going to use now," Dr Grayson continued. "Our plan is to put Paul into an induced coma. Coma is a frightening word, I know, but all that we mean by 'induced coma' is that we will put Paul more deeply to sleep. We will be able to wake him up when we feel that he is ready. This will give his body time to mend itself. When we wake him, he will be in a far better state to undergo the tests needed to assess his mental state."

"Are there dangers to doing this?" Jo asked.

"David and I both believe there are greater dangers if we do not do this."

"How long will he be in this 'induced coma?'" There were tears in Jo's eyes.

"It's hard to say with any certainty," David Portman answered. "Much will depend on how quickly his body heals. My best guess is one or two weeks."

Jo gasped.

"You will, of course, be able to visit him – to sit with him and touch him and talk to him. In fact, we would urge you to do all of those things. The other major bonus is that Paul will be pain free during this time and, by the time we wake him, his physical injuries will be healed to the extent that he will not experience too much pain from them at all."

"Why did you feel the need to consult with me over this treatment?" Jo suddenly asked. "Why didn't you just go ahead if it's so obviously the right thing to do?"

Dr. Grayson answered. "There are always unknowns involved, especially with a patient who has suffered such serious injuries as Paul. There is a risk in this course of action but, as I said before, we think there is an even greater risk if we just allow Paul to struggle with waking up himself. David and I wanted to let you know our plans and hear your comments and concerns. We all have to work as a team, and you are an important part of that team. We would not dream of inducing coma without first explaining to you what was involved."

Jo looked at Sally and then back towards the two doctors. "It would be very silly of me to disagree with you. You have Paul's best interests at heart, and I thank you for being so open and honest with me. Of course you must do whatever you feel is best for Paul. You can do so with my full understanding and consent."

"Thank you Jo," Portman said. "Why don't you pop in and see Paul now and then come back tomorrow. By then, you will be able to touch him and talk to him. I'm sure that will make you feel a lot better."

"You will still ring me if there is any change, won't you? I'll leave Sally's number with Ellie. I have a mobile that I can give her as well."

"That goes without saying. This really is the best way forwards."

The two men left the waiting room.

Ellie came in and offered to take Jo and Sally to see Paul.

"You go," Sally said. "I'll wait here for you. Take your time."

They drove from the hospital straight back to Sally's house. The conversation on the way home had left them both feeling positive about what they had been told.

Jo seemed to be more relaxed – just having a plan of action and a timescale helped so much. She would not be spending every minute of every hour on edge: waiting for the phone to ring, wondering if Paul had woken up, dreading how he would be feeling. For the first time in many hours, Jo felt capable of getting on with things, safe in the knowledge that the doctors were in full control of Paul's situation. She even felt hungry.

After having a cup of coffee, Jo decided to pop home and put a few bits and pieces in a case to bring round for her stay.

"If you're feeling up to it, let's go out somewhere this afternoon," Sally suggested. "Maybe we'll go out and get some lunch somewhere nice. One bacon roll isn't going to keep you going for long."

"That sounds good. Won't be long. How about food for the house? I've got a fridge and a freezer full of stuff at home that will have to get eaten. I can bring some round."

"Don't bother right now," Sally laughed. "There's plenty here. We can raid your cupboards later. Just grab the essentials and come back round. I'll have a think about where we can go."

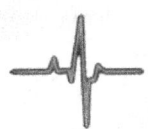

Chapter 9

Portman and Grayson hoped that the steps that they had taken would help to quiet the activity in Paul's bruised and swollen brain, and initial readings had been good. Electrodes attached to Paul's head carried tiny impulses that were translated into multi-coloured lines that danced across another monitor. During the many moments when Paul had tried to wake, this screen had become a confusion of jagged activity – too much activity for the doctors.

Now, those sharp jagged lines had become a series of smoother waves. Paul's brain was still active, but whatever was going on in there was, at least, less frantic and less worrying.

"Bloody idiot," Paul mouthed to the young driver of the black Audi Coupe who had cruised alongside him in the outside lane of the M6, but was refusing to complete his overtaking manoeuvre.

The reaction from inside the other car was a silly grin and a derogatory hand gesture that infuriated Paul even more.

The black Audi then slowed and moved in close behind Paul with headlights flashing.

For several miles the two cars drove in perfect formation - the black car mimicking every move that Paul made at a distance of only a few metres behind. Accelerate...brake...change lane...the black car followed Paul's every move.

Once again, the black Audi moved out to overtake, but once alongside, the driver held his position and looked across at Paul with the same silly grin. Slower moving traffic in the inside lane meant that Paul could not move there. A glance in the rear view mirror showed another car following closely, so Paul could not risk braking to shake off the Audi.

The road ahead was fairly clear. Temper got the better of him and Paul floored the accelerator.

His own Audi moved smoothly away...90...100...110 miles per hour. The exhilaration of speed hit him. The engine purred and he knew there was still more power if he needed it.

He checked his mirrors for the black car. No need. It was there – just on his shoulder with headlights flashing. "This is bloody crazy," Paul thought to himself. "The guy's a maniac – we're both going to end up in the crash barriers."

Glancing in the rear-view mirror, Paul knew nothing was close behind now – not surprising at his speed.

He noticed signs for a junction in one mile's distance and made his decision.

As he passed the 300-yard marker for the junction, he checked the position of the black car. It was still there on his shoulder.

He drifted across to the inside lane and braked fiercely. The mouth of the junction was there and he managed to make the turn leaving the black Audi stranded on the motorway, disappearing into the distance.

"Bye-bye!" Paul smiled to himself. "Go and have your accident, you moron. Didn't see that move coming, did you?"

Paul had no idea where he was. He glanced at his watch: 8.30pm. Daylight was fading. A sign for a lay by caught his eye and he decided to pulled in and ring Jo.

"Hi there!" Jo said. "I was hoping you'd call. How did it go? Did you get the part?"

"It went fantastically. Won't know for a few days if I've got it but I'm very hopeful, judged on the comments I got. I tried to ring a couple of hours ago but you were out and your mobile was off. You know I'm a good boy and I don't try phoning when I'm driving."

"Yeah...right! Anyhow, what time will you be home? I'm dying to hear all about your day."

"Actually, I'm not quite sure where I am."

Paul told Jo about his encounter with the black Audi Coupe, which explained why he wasn't sure where he had left the motorway. "I can see a junction not far down the road with some signposts. It's getting on for 9pm. And I'm really shattered. Would you mind if I found a B&B or a motel and got back first thing tomorrow? Tomorrow's Saturday so we can have the whole weekend to chat about what's going to happen when I do get the part. If I drive home now, it will be very late by the time I get back. You'll probably be in bed anyhow."

"Oh Honey! I just want to give you a cuddle and a 'well done' kiss. I can wait up for you."

"Tell you what," Paul said, "I'll find out exactly where I am and how long it would take to drive home. I'll call you again and let you know what I'm doing. I want to cuddle you too, you know!"

They agreed, and Paul pulled out of the lay by and headed for the junction that he had seen.

The place names on the signposts at the junction meant nothing to Paul. To the left and right, the roads were unlit single tracks. Daylight had gone. Rydon was two miles according to the left-hand sign; Brookham was three miles to the right.

Paul chose Rydon as it was closest. He just wanted a drink and some food and to find out where he was.

The narrow road twisted between thick hedges that edged open fields. The Audi's headlights glared in the deepening gloom.

As Paul rounded another sharp bend, he saw a building on the left side of the road – the first building he had encountered. He slowed the car and was happy to see the sign for a pub hanging from a post. "The Chair," it read. "Rooms Available - Good Food."

He pulled the Audi onto the gravelled car park and got out.

The Chair looked welcoming enough – an old stone building with leaded windows and walls that were almost entirely covered with sweet-smelling honeysuckle and dark ivy. Lights shone from two large ground-floor rooms separated by a single, small, arched doorway. The second-story windows were all in darkness, save one at the extreme left of the building.

Paul's Audi was the only car in the car park – not a good sign. But he made his way towards the arched doorway and stepped inside.

What had appeared, from the outside, to be two downstairs rooms turned out to be one large area.

A bar ran the whole length of the room, bearing several sets of beer pulls and bowls of nuts and snacks. Behind the bar was the usual display of glasses and bottles together with numerous polished brasses and other ornaments.

At the far end of the room was a massive open fireplace and stone chimney. Flames danced from a huge log that was burning in the hearth.

As he surveyed his surroundings, Paul suddenly realised that the place was packed, with hardly an empty table. Drinkers lined the bar. Food was being served at place-laid tables to his left. To his right (where the fireplace stood), the tables were uncovered but for the accustomed beer mats. In the corner, next to the fire, was an enormous armchair, upholstered in what appeared to be aging red leather. Though he could only see the profile of the man who was sitting in the chair, Paul had a distinct sense of recognition.

Paul wondered where all the people had come from as he walked to the bar. Not a single car outside and, in the mile or so he had driven, he had not seen a single building – yet the pub was heaving with activity.

A grey-haired barman noticed Paul and approached with a welcoming smile. "Good evening, sir! And what can I get you?"

Paul explained that he was lost and would also like something to eat.

"Better sort out the food first," the barman said with grin. "We stop taking orders at 9pm and it's a bit past that already, but I'll see if we can make an exception for a lost and weary traveller. The menu's up there on the board. I can recommend the Steak and Ale Pie - had some myself tonight."

"Steak and Ale Pie's fine," Paul said.

"Would that be with chips or just some green veg?"

"Chips and vegetables would be great, and a pint of your best bitter, please."

"Give me two ticks and I'll get that ordered for you."

The barman disappeared through a door at the end of the bar, leaving Paul to take in the scene around the room. Once again, he looked toward the man sitting in the armchair, but with people constantly moving in his line of vision it was impossible to get a clear look at the man's face.

He was still peering through the crowd when the barman returned.

"It'll be about ten minutes," he said. "If you'd like to find a table, I'll bring your drink over."

"Tell you what," Paul said, "hold the drink until the meal is ready. I want to phone home, so I'll pop outside where it's less noisy. By the way, do you have a room free just for tonight? I think I might stay if you do."

"No problem. We haven't got anyone staying tonight as far as I know. You'll be very welcome."

Paul went out to the car park and phoned Jo on his mobile. Though he still hadn't discovered exactly where he was, he started by saying "Looks like I'm still north of Lancaster, love – well over two hours from home. I've found a nice Old-World pub and ordered some food. They have a spare room too, so I think I'll just stay for the night and set out for home first thing in the morning...if that's okay."

Jo didn't argue, though her tone told Paul that she was disappointed.

"The pub's called The Chair. It's about a mile from a place called Rydon. Give me a call on my mobile if you need me. I'll make sure that I leave it on. Sleep tight, Jo. See you in the morning. I'll give you a ring before I set out so you'll know what time to expect me."

—⋀—

Paul went back inside the bar. He caught the eye of the barman and indicated that he was going to find a table on the restaurant end of the room. The barman waved an acknowledgement.

When the barman brought his pint to the table, Paul asked him about the lack of cars in the car park.

"Where have all these people come from? Don't tell me everybody walks around here."

"They're mostly regulars." the barman said, "Guess I know most of them by name. Do you know, I've never really though about how they get here – just happy that they do, I suppose."

"If you know them all," Paul asked, "can you tell me who the guy sitting in the red armchair is?"

Without even turning to look the barman said, "There's no one in the armchair, sir. No one ever sits there. Bit of a tale about that old chair, but we don't talk about it. The pub's named after it, you know."

"But there's a man sitting there now...at least there was. I had the distinct feeling that I knew him – that's why I asked."

Both men stood and looked towards the far end of the bar.

"Just like I said," the barman stated. "Chair's empty!"

Paul looked around to see if he could recognise the man he had seen in the chair at another table or at the bar, but he could not be sure. No one in the room looked familiar.

"Must've gone," Paul mused, "though I don't recall anybody leaving, and I'm right next to the door. Anyhow, tell me where I am – I'm still lost. Where's the nearest town that I'll know of?"

Before the barman had time to answer, Paul's meal arrived.

"You enjoy your food," the barman said as he turned to leave the table. "Did you want that room for the night?"

Paul said that he did intend to stay and was told that his room would be prepared.

"You'll be in number 4 – top of the stairs and second door on the right. That pie looks lovely. Think I'll have some more for my supper."

───┤├───

The food was first class and the beer was delicious. Paul ordered a second pint at the table. By the time he had finished, the large room was still packed full. Paul made his way back to the bar to get one more pint before going to bed. The grey-haired barman was nowhere to be seen, but the girl who had waited on him at his table appeared behind the bar and asked if she could get him anything.

"Just one more pint, please. And I guess you'll want me to sign in if I'm staying here tonight."

He was presented with a registration card together with his pint of bitter.

"Just fill it in and leave it on the bar," the girl said. "I'll pick it up as soon as I've been to the kitchen. You're room 4 – top of the stairs, second door on the right. Sleep tight."

Paul filled in the card. Though he took a while enjoying his third pint, neither the waitress nor the barman returned. Through the restaurant, Paul noticed a flight of stairs and assumed they would lead to his bedroom. He took a final look around the room – the armchair was empty.

With somewhat troubled thoughts, Paul headed for the stairs.

Number 4 was a small, but adequate, room looking out over the car park. His own white Audi Coupe was the only vehicle to be seen. A mist had formed and visibility was restricted to no further than the far side of the single-track road that had brought him to The Chair.

He lay on the double bed and stared at the ceiling.

"Where am I?" he thought, realising he still hadn't established his whereabouts.

He considered phoning Jo, but when he looked at his watch, he decided against it. Instead, still fully clothed, he closed his eyes. Unanswered questions filled his mind. Not only "Where am I?" but "Where did all those people come from? Why no other cars? Who was in the armchair? What was the story of the armchair that nobody talked about?"

Confused and slightly perturbed, Paul drifted into a troubled sleep.

He awoke with a start. The room was in darkness. He fumbled for the bedside lamp and sent his mobile phone crashing to the floor from the small table next to his bed. He stared at his watch whilst trying to get his head together. The watch read 5.20am. Paul began to remember the happenings of the last ten hours.

He realised that he was sweating, not because he was too warm, but a cold sweat brought on by fear. And then it hit him. It couldn't possibly be true. There was no way that it could be – yet his mind was certain...chillingly certain. The profile of the face he had seen in the red armchair was the same one he had seen from the driver's seat of his car as he had looked across at the black Audi racing along the motorway a few hours ago.

The wavy lines across the hospital monitor suddenly changed to a haphazard series of needle-sharp peaks and troughs. The heart rate monitor gave out a series of shrill warning bleeps. Kathy rushed into the room and immediately paged for help.

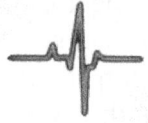

Chapter 10

Jo threw some underwear and a single change of clothes into a small case. She added some toiletries and the book she was reading. Downstairs, she grabbed her laptop and a lightweight waterproof hoodie and put the collection next to the front door.

In the kitchen, she quickly rinsed the few cups and plates that were sitting in the sink. Finally, she checked the fridge for anything that might spoil. She then checked the other rooms to make sure that everything was switched off and that the doors and windows were still locked. She chided herself mentally for being so meticulous. "You're only going round the corner, woman! You'll probably be popping in here two or three times a day. For God's sake – just leave everything as it is and go!"

She was about to close the front door behind her when she suddenly decided to update the message on the answer phone so that people could find her in an emergency. She changed the message to include her mobile number, but made sure to say nothing about being away for a few days – that would be an open invitation to burglars.

"Must remember to leave my mobile on at all times," she thought, which prompted her to rummage for the phone charger that lived in the kitchen drawers.

She opened the front door again and then went back to the living room and switched on a small table light, so that, at night, it would look as if someone was home.

At last, she closed the front door behind her and set off round the corner to Sally's.

Sally had put on a housecoat and was drinking more coffee. "I must close my eyes for an hour before we do anything else, Jo. I'm shattered!"

"Sorry Sal, How totally thoughtless of me. You go and get some sleep. I'll just potter about. We can go out and find something to eat later, if you feel like it. I might pop into town on the bus whilst you're asleep. I promised Dad that I'd see about hiring a car."

"Don't be daft, Jo," Sally said. "I'll only need an hour. I'm used to getting by on a quick kip here and there – comes with the job. Wake me up at four and we'll still have plenty of time to get to town and sort out transport for you before we eat. You just make yourself at home. Put the telly on or something. Have a mooch through my music collection – there's bound to be something there that you like. Help yourself to a drink or a snack. There's plenty in the kitchen."

Jo spent the next hour and a half getting accustomed to her new surroundings. She started in the kitchen, peering in cupboards and drawers and finding out where everything was. She made tea for herself.

She carried her drink through to the small front room and sat on the comfy sofa in front of the television. She thumbed through a few magazines that were lying on the coffee table.

She wished that Sally had shown her to her room so that she could have had nap too. After a while, she took her laptop and keyed in the site for her personal banking. When she finally reached her account, her jaw dropped. Mitch had transferred £5000 into her bank. She immediately took her mobile and called her father-in-law.

"Dad, what's all this money for? You shouldn't have. I don't need it."

"Hey, calm down, honey," Mitch said. "There's no point in me putting a bit of money in today and a bit next week and so on and so on. We don't know how much you'll need. The car hire will be quite expensive for a start. It's there now, Jo, so use it – please! It's petty cash to me, but it might make all the difference to you. What's the point of me sitting here worrying whether you've got enough money?"

"It's just the amount, Dad. It's too much – I feel dreadful. Paul would have a fit. You know how independent he is."

"Right now, it's none of his business. Please don't feel bad. Your mum and I just want to make sure that you are alright. We love you, honey. Now, forget the damn money – is there any more news from the hospital?"

Jo explained about Sally and the meeting with doctors Portman and Grayson, about the plan to put Paul into an induced coma and about staying with Sally for a few days.

Mitch sounded relieved on all counts. He was quick to point out that just knowing what was happening with Paul would mean that she could relax a little. He was delighted that she had found a friend to stay with for company through such a difficult time. The call ended with both of them feeling relieved.

At four o'clock, Jo was about to wake Sally with a cup of tea when Sally walked into the kitchen, dressed and ready to go.

"Wow! That's impressive. When I go to sleep, it takes an earthquake to wake me. You sure you're okay?"

"Built-in alarm clock," Sally joked. "As I said, it all goes with the job. I'm fine – refreshed and ready for anything."

The two of them drove into town. Their first stop was a large Europcar depot, where they negotiated a deal on a small hatchback for a period of one month and arranged for the vehicle to be delivered to Jo's house at 9am the next morning, where it could be parked in the drive until needed.

Next, Sally needed a few essentials from the supermarket. Jo wanted to pay; they finally agreed to share the bill.

"I'm starving!" Sally grumbled as they left the supermarket. "How about you?"

"Yes, I could eat something."

They decided on a pub-style carvery on the outskirts of town.

"This I am paying for!" Jo insisted as they enjoyed their meal. "You've been so kind, Sal. It's my treat to say 'thank you,' and I don't want to hear any argument."

Over coffee, Jo said that she was going to call Kathy at the hospital, just to see if there had been any developments. The time it took to connect the call was longer than the conversation. Kathy confirmed that the induced coma had been started and that Paul was sleeping peacefully. There were no immediate concerns. Kathy suggested that Jo should visit tomorrow, when she would be able to sit with Paul and talk to him.

Sally watched in silence as Jo was speaking. She couldn't help noticing the tears that were forming in Jo's eyes; she reached across the table to hold Jo's hand.

When the call ended, Jo explained what she had been told and Sally comforted her.

"It's going to be okay. Paul's going to be fine. You have to keep believing. It's the only thing you can do that will help. When you sit with him and talk to him, you have to sound cheerful. Your voice has to be normal and positive not depressed and weepy. It's so easy for me to say, and I know it's so hard for you to do, but you can do it, Jo. You can do it for Paul. Just remember, love, Paul wouldn't want you to be unhappy – that's the last thing he'd want."

Jo knew that every word Sally said made perfect sense, but knowing that didn't make her feel any better.

"Let's just have a quite evening in front of the telly or listen to some music," Sally suggested. "I'm at work tomorrow afternoon, but I'll come with you to the hospital in the morning if you like. I'll be with you to give you a bit of moral support when you sit with Paul for the first time. I can hardly imagine what you're going through, but you know you can lean on me."

"Thanks, Sal. Yes, I'd like you to be with me when I see Paul. I'm not too sure how I'll react. I'm just so scared."

As they drove back to Sally's house, they passed Jo's. Daylight was fading. Sally parked in the street in front of her own home.

"Sal," Jo said, "I'm just going to pop home for a minute. I left a light on in the living room before I came round, just so that it would look as if someone was in. When we drove past just now, I could have sworn no light was on."

"I'm coming with you. Probably just a bulb gone, but you never know. Best to take the strong arm of the law with you while you have the chance."

Jo smiled.

When they reached Jo's house, it was obvious from outside that no lights were on in the living room. Jo opened the front door and Sally went in first.

Everything appeared untouched except for the small lamp Jo had left switched on. It lay on the floor beside the low table where it had sat. The bulb was smashed, and shards of glass littering the wooden floor.

Jo stood stunned as Sally methodically checked other rooms. As she stared at the broken lamp, she noticed the circular grey stain on the polished wood. It was faint and fading fast – but it was definitely there. "Sally!" Jo yelled, "Quick, come here!"

Sally was by her side in a flash.

"Look! Look at the floor! That grey stain there – do you see it?"

Sally knelt down and looked, but the circle of grey had almost disappeared. "I can't see anything."

"It was there! I saw it distinctly – just like when the picture got broken. Now it has faded away. You think I'm going mad, don't you? I'm not mad, Sally – it was there. I swear it!"

"I believe that you did see it," Sally said, putting a comforting arm round Jo's shoulders. "But I also believe that maybe your mind wanted to see it for some reason. Pressure does strange things to us all. I know you're telling me exactly what you saw, but it's gone now. Let's find a bulb for the lamp and clear up this glass. We'll leave the lamp on again. We can pop round and check that it's still on later, if you like. My guess is that the bulb blew and that the explosion toppled the lamp off the table."

Jo's logical mind told her that Sally was probably right. They cleared the mess and reset the lamp, which was working perfectly.

"Know what?" Sally asked. "I've just realised that I haven't even shown you to your room. How rude of me! I know you saw it when I first showed you the house, but I should have taken you there and settled you in before I had my sleep. Sorry, Jo."

"It's fine," Jo replied. "Why don't you show me now and we can settle down for a quiet night. I'm okay now. Sorry if I shouted at you. I'm just a bit on edge."

Sally and Jo left the house and made their way back round the corner.

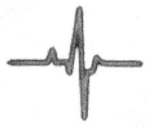

Chapter 11

Monday at the police station had been manic, as usual.

The weekend's incidents were reviewed and given an order of importance. The fatal accident on the M6 Motorway on Saturday night was placed fairly low on the list.

A team of accident investigators, led by Sgt Josh Brooks, had visited the scene of the crash looking for evidence to help them understand exactly what had happened.

There had been no real eyewitnesses. First on the scene had been a lorry driver, who had been overtaken by the two speeding Audis and, in his own words, had "sort of seen them coming together in the far distance."

He had stopped at the scene of the accident and called the emergency services. A car carrying three medical students had also stopped.

They had split into two pairs, the lorry driver and one student going to the black Audi, the other two students running down the embankment to the white one.

The driver of the black Audi was obviously dead.

At the other car, one of the students had lain flat on the ground and reached inside the overturned vehicle. To his utter amazement, he could feel a faint pulse in the driver's bloody neck.

He shouted up to the other two men that this driver was still alive and to get the ambulance crew to the white car as quickly as possible.

Within minutes of being alerted, ambulance, police and firemen had arrived on the scene in that order.

All attention was directed to the white Audi; even so, it had taken nearly forty minutes to free the driver from the twisted mess.

The lorry driver had reported that traffic was light on the southbound carriageway where he and the Audis were travelling, but northbound traffic was much heavier. It was entirely possible that someone on the far side of the motorway could have seen the accident more clearly, despite it being dark. The carriageway lighting at that point on the road was fairly good.

Incident boards were set up on both sides of the motorway, asking for any witnesses to the crash to come forward.

Josh Brooks' inspection of the two vehicles didn't reveal much that wasn't already known. The two cars had definitely hit each other. The black Audi had white paint in heavy gouges behind the passenger side door - the white Audi showed damage with black paint embedded on its front, driver's side corner, around the headlamp area.

Brooks concluded that the black car had been in the outside lane of the motorway and to the right of the white Audi. The black Audi must have swerved across the front of the other car. Contact had occurred and the two vehicles had ploughed, in unison, through the same spot in the barriers and into the fields beyond. The black car had gone straight on into a solid horse chestnut tree, while the white car had careened to the left and rolled end over end down a steep embankment, coming to rest on its roof nearly eighty metres away. Tyre marks on the motorway tarmac had indicated the extreme speed at which the cars were travelling when they lost control.

Why there weren't two dead bodies, Josh couldn't quite understand.

Once Josh and his team finished their inspection, both vehicles were taken to a local scrap-yard. For the time being, both cars were impounded under police jurisdiction, just in case further evidence came to hand. They were also available for insurance assessors to view, should they think it necessary.

Statements were taken from the lorry driver, the three medical students, and the emergency services personnel who had attended the scene.

All that remained, for the time being anyway, was for Josh to write his report and file it.

In that report, he noted that the emergency services had praised the efforts of the lorry driver and the students and were sure that the surviving driver undoubtedly owed his life to their bravery and quick thinking.

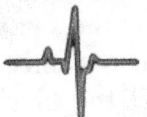

Chapter 12

Paul's mind was racing. No matter how much he tried to convince himself that the face in the chair and the face in the black Audi were not one and the same, he couldn't. The more he thought, the more certain he became.

Was it possible that the black Audi could have beaten him to the pub? If so, was it just a coincidence that the two men had both chosen to frequent the same establishment? Did the man in the Audi know him from somewhere? Perhaps he misunderstood the man's motives. Did he want not to race but just to talk? No, that scenario didn't work. If the guy just wanted to talk, he would have come over and introduced himself when Paul came into the bar.

Paul paced the small room. He stood at the window looking out into the approaching dawn. Open countryside greeted him – nothing but fields and trees with no noticeable landmarks. Nothing to catch the eye.

He was certain the black Audi had not followed him down the motorway exit. He had only just been able to make the turn himself and he had seen the other car speeding away. Paul needed a map. How far was the next motorway junction?

He tried to remember how long he had talked to Jo on the phone from the lay by that he'd stopped in. No more than 5 minutes at the maximum, he concluded.

It was just possible that if there were another turn off the motorway within a couple of miles that linked to the same road to Rydon, the black Audi could have made it to The Chair before him. Unlikely…but he would have to check.

"Hold on a minute," he suddenly thought. "This is all garbage. If the Audi *had* beaten me to the pub, where was the bloody car? It wasn't on the car park!"

Maybe the guy had parked round the back or something? "For Christ's sake man, you've just had a nightmare – wake up!"

But he was awake, and it was the same man – he knew it. God, how he wished he weren't so certain!

Paul gathered his few belongings at 6am. He left enough cash on the bedside table to pay for the room and went downstairs. A woman was laying the restaurant tables for breakfast. "Don't know why she's bothering," Paul thought. "I'm the only resident."

He told the woman he had left money for his room and to please explain that he needed to leave early. If there was a balance to pay, the landlord had his phone number on the registration card. The woman seemed totally uninterested in what he was saying, and simply opened the one and only door for him to leave.

It was too early to call Jo. He decided to set off towards home and call her from a services area when he stopped for breakfast.

Paul turned right out of the car park and headed for the junction that would take him back onto the M6. He would soon know how far it was to the next turn off and if it was remotely possible that the black Audi could have got to The Chair before him.

He was suddenly aware that he was constantly checking his rear view mirror – something that he would normally do without thinking. But this morning was different. Was he expecting the black Audi to cruise up behind him and for the previous evening's events to begin all over again?

The motorway, in front of and behind him, was quiet – just the odd vehicle here and there. No black Audis!

He had been driving for nearly fifteen minutes when he saw a blue and white sign for a junction. As he read the sign, once again his heart started pumping.

"Junction 12 Cannock," it read.

"Bloody impossible!" Paul thought. "I'm nearly home – no more than half an hour away. What's happening to me? I thought I was still up in the Lake District when I stopped last night. I can't have been this close to home. I can't have driven nearly 150 miles without realising." Paul's concentration was blown. "Got to stop at the next services at Hilton Park and think."

As Paul approached Junction 11, the Cheslyn Hay turn off, he saw police cars and recovery vehicles stopped on the hard shoulder. Paul slowed the car. He could see a break in the crash barriers and dark skid marks on the tarmac. He could see a black vehicle standing almost on its nose against a tree.

"A *black* vehicle!" His mind froze.

The hospital monitor spiked madly. Paul was panicking again.

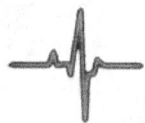

Chapter 13

Jo and Sally had spent a quiet evening watching a movie and sometimes chatting.

Thoughtful Sally had found an extension for the house telephone and placed the set on Jo's bedside table, just in case there was a call from the hospital in the night.

Jo had gone to bed early feeling totally drained, but found that her mind would not let her body rest. She could not help lingering on the incident with the table lamp and that grey stain on the floor again – could it really be just a trick of light? She thought not.

The anticipation of the following day's hospital visit terrified her. How would she feel when she sat at Paul's bedside and touched his beaten body for the first time since the accident? How would she manage to talk to his sleeping form without breaking down? She tried to mentally steel herself for the moment, but knew in her heart that she would probably fail.

Then there was the future to think about - how her life would be impacted, depending on how full Paul's eventual recovery would be. The various scenarios spun around and around in her head, most of them too dreadful to contemplate.

It seemed that she had hardly slept at all when Sally touched her arm and presented her with a mug of tea. Outside, it was raining again.

"Best get yourself up and going," Sally said cheerfully, "You'll have to be round at your place in half an hour. The hire car will be arriving and there's bound to be paperwork to sign. Did you sleep okay?"

Jo lied in the affirmative and thanked Sally for the tea.

Jo had only been in her house for a couple of minutes when the doorbell rang. The guy from Europcar was standing there, smiling and dangling a set of keys from his hand. He asked her to have a quick check of the car and then demonstrated some of the main controls, indicators, lights and wipers, et cetera. Jo signed the paper that he presented to her and he was gone. She left the car in the driveway and walked back round to Sally's house.

"Everything alright?" Sally enquired.

Jo told her that the car was fine and that they could use it to go to the hospital, but Sally insisted on taking them in her car.

"It's going to be a pretty traumatic day, I would guess," Sally said, "Best I do the driving. So, how do you feel about breakfast? You really must try to eat – even if you don't really feel like it."

Jo was surprised to find she was starving and offered to cook for the two of them.

"I've got a better idea. Let's go to the all-night café that I told you about – you know, the one I got the bacon rolls from when I came round yesterday morning. It's sort of on the way to the hospital and they do breakfasts to die for."

An hour later, Jo was pleased she had agreed. The breakfast had been massive and magnificent.

"How can you eat like that and still have a catwalk figure?" Sally laughed. "Look at me: everything I eat is instantly transformed into inches around the waist or other undesirable places!"

As they entered I.C. Unit 3 at the hospital, Jo was beginning to wish that she hadn't eaten so well. Her stomach was churning.

To Jo's relief, they were met by Kathy. Jo had instantly liked Kathy. Ellie was fine too, but she could, at times, seem a little abrupt. Kathy was more supportive, more sympathetic, easier to talk to, and easier to break down in front of; Jo had the feeling that the latter would be needed.

"Give us ten minutes," Kathy said, as they sat in the waiting room. "The doctors are with Paul just now, but they won't be long – just routine checks. As soon as they're done, I'll come and get you."

Jo wanted to tell Kathy how tentative she was feeling and that she was worried about how she would react to being close to Paul, but instead she just smiled and said okay.

As they were waiting, the door of the room opened and Dr. Grayson came in. Instantly recognising the concern on Jo's face, the doctor quickly assured them that everything was fine with Paul and that he just wanted to have a few words about what was going on.

Jo braced herself.

"Paul is now in a very deep sleep. From a physical point of view, this is fine. David, sorry, that's Dr.Portman, is more than happy with the way that his body is recovering and we can safely say that he is out of immediate danger in that respect. The mental side of his condition is still unclear and will probably remain so until we wake him.

"I am a little ..." he paused. "I was going to use the word 'perturbed,' but that would give the wrong impression. Let's put it this way: I'm surprised at the amount of activity still going on in Paul's brain despite his deep sleep. I would have expected the activity to settle down, but that doesn't seem to be the case – at least for some of the time. The positive side is that his brain is functioning. It would be far more worrying if we saw too little activity. I'm going to accompany you when you go in to see Paul so that I can have a look at his reaction to you being there. I expect there will be little or no indication that he knows you are with him, but you never can tell.

"I know how difficult this first meeting is going to be for you; you must not worry if you get upset in there. I will tell you if there is any adverse reaction from Paul, but that is highly unlikely. Just try to ignore me and Kathy, and concentrate on Paul. By all means, hold his hand and talk to him. Stay for as long or as short a time as you wish. No one will blame you if your emotions take over.

"Are you ready to see him now, or would you like to take a few minutes?"

"I think I'm as ready as I'm ever going to be," Jo said, her voice trembling. "I'll try my best to keep my emotions in check and, if I can't, I'll just come out for a little while until I can get control again."

Jo, Sally and the doctor left the waiting room and headed for Paul's bedside.

A chair for Jo to sit in had been placed by the side of the bed. Kathy had arranged for another chair for Sally to be put at the back of the room.

As Jo sat down, she felt overcome by the magnitude of the moment. She stared at Paul – at the tubes and wires and bandages. He lay flat on his back, his head slightly raised and his arms by his sides, on top of the white sheets.

She moved her hand towards his arm and then took it away again, not daring to touch him.

After several long moments, her fingers reached Paul's hand and a shiver went through her whole body. She wanted to withdraw, but couldn't.

Jo turned to look at Sally, who smiled her support and encouragement back in Jo's direction.

"Hi, Paul. It's Jo," she whispered, half expecting his eyes to open in recognition.

Though Jo didn't see it, the lines on the screen that monitored Paul's brain activity leapt, and then almost immediately settled back into their rhythmic wavy pattern.

All the fear left Jo, and she found the inner strength to deal with the situation – a strength she could never have believed was inside her. She began to talk, quite calmly, to Paul. She squeezed his hand gently. She watched his face. A feeling of absolute peace came over her. It was in that moment that she somehow knew she would get her Paul back – whole and healthy.

Tears welled in her eyes but, to her amazement, they were tears of joy. She stayed with Paul for almost half an hour, telling him news, comforting him, and even chiding him at one stage for leaving dirty socks under the bed. It was as if there were no one else in the room.

Eventually, she said that she would have to go but assured him that she would be back again soon. She wanted to kiss him, but his facial bandages made that impossible. Instead, she bent and kissed his hand.

Outside Paul's room, Jo let out a huge sigh and turned to give Sally a hug.

"Well done, girl!" Sally said, almost in tears herself, "You were so brave in there. How are you feeling? If you want to spend more time with Paul, I can pick you up later."

Jo declined, saying she would visit longer tomorrow, when Sally was back at work. "I'm fine. And Paul's going to be fine. I just know it, Sally. I'm starving. Our little breakfast seems a long time ago. What do you say to me buying us lunch? On Dad, of course!"

Sally rubbed her stomach and grimaced. "More inches!" she groaned. "But what the hell!"

The two of them left the hospital, arm in arm.

Doctor Grayson said nothing about the reaction he had noticed when Jo touched Paul. He thought that to do so might inhibit Jo when she next visited. There would be plenty of time to assess and to discuss Paul's responses.

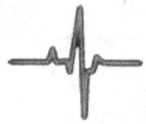

Chapter 14

His mind still in a daze, Paul pulled in to the Hilton Park service area.

He made for the washrooms and ran the tap until the water was icy cold. He cupped his hands to catch the water, he splashed his face. He leaned on the basin and looked at himself in the mirror. The unshaven face that looked back at him was drained of all colour and emotion. Staring eyes, mouth set firmly, hair uncombed. Paul looked away.

He made his way to the coffee shop and ordered black coffee from a middle-aged woman who looked almost as blank as he felt. The area was quiet at this hour of the morning – just a couple of truckers, tucking into their greasy breakfasts. Paul chose a table by the large windows and sat down.

He rubbed his eyes in an attempt to wake himself from the nightmare that he was going through. It didn't help. Six packets of sugar went into his paper cup of coffee. It needed at least six to become drinkable.

Paul took a deep breath and willed himself to think back, rationally, over all that had happened since he first saw the black Audi Coupe last evening.

The sequence of events was crystal clear in his mind right up to the moment he had seen the motorway sign that read, "Junction 12 – Cannock." He couldn't possibly be that far down the motorway. Where had the last 150 miles gone? And the black car that was crumpled against a tree – could it really the black Audi? Maybe he should go back and check.

"Idiot!" he told himself. "Look at a bloody map!"

He left his half-finished coffee on the table and walked briskly to the shop; grabbing a map and a morning paper, he returned to his window seat.

He spread the map on the table. His finger traced the route of the M6 motorway.

"Okay – I left The Chair and joined the motorway within less than two miles. The next junction was Junction 12, so Junction 13 must be the one for The Chair. Let's see. Here's Junction 13, so this must be the road that leads down to the T-junction with Rydon to the left and.... What was the other name? *Brook* something to the right."

As he talked to himself, his fingers followed the roads on the map.

"This is madness!" he thought. "There's no T–junction. No Rydon. The road goes on straight for miles into Stafford."

Paul realised he had bought a map of just the M6 motorway winding its way from the Midlands to the Scottish border. Paul made his way back to the shop and picked up a U.K. Atlas. He thumbed quickly through the index at the back of the book looking for the place name of Rydon. Just one entry was shown – Rydon, Devon Map 58 E7.

"Wonderful!" Paul thought. "Now I've lost a whole bloody town! It was *Rydon,* wasn't it? Or have I got the name wrong? No – it was definitely Rydon. What the hell is going on?"

Back at his table, Paul folded the map. He glanced at the front page of his newspaper. What was left of his coffee was stone cold. He ordered another and sat back down.

He again thought he should call Jo. When he glanced at his watch, it was just after 7.15am. "Give her another few minutes in bed," he told himself. "Have your coffee and then call. There has to be a reasonable explanation for all this. Just chill for a few minutes."

Paul flicked through the morning paper without really seeing any of its contents. Turning the final page, he casually glanced outside and saw the figure of a man standing with his back to the window.

As Paul looked out, the man slowly turned his head and smiled.

The half full cup of coffee fell from Paul's grasp. His stomach heaved – he could taste the bile in his throat.

In Paul's hospital room, all hell broke loose – piercing warning bleeps rang out, lights flashed, jagged lined bounced from top to bottom of monitor screens, and nurses and doctors rushed to the scene.

Chapter 15

Jo rang the hospital early the next morning.

Before she had time to ask how Paul was, the voice on the other end of the line informed her that Dr. Grayson wished to talk to her and said that she was being transferred. Jo waited anxiously.

Her worries halved when she heard Dr.Grayson's cheerful greeting.

"Good morning, Mrs Ford. You saved me a call. I was about to get in touch with you."

"Is Paul okay? Has something happened?"

"We had a bit of a scare in the night – but before you start worrying, everything is under control and Paul's fine."

"What happened?" Jo enquired.

"Paul had another one of his bad dreams that set a few alarm bells ringing in his room. He's perfectly settled again now. Are you coming in to see him today? I'd like a chat with you. I'm here until about midday."

"I'll come straight over."

"Just have a think if you know of anything in Paul's life that may be causing these dreams – anything that he might be anxious or worried about, anything that he might be afraid of. Something is going on inside his head that is causing these panic attacks. See if you can come up with anything that may help us understand. No need to hurry to get here. Let the morning rush-hour traffic thin out."

"Alright. I'll be there about 10.30."

"One more thing, Mrs Ford. If I'm not around when you arrive, please ask the nurses to find me. I'd appreciate it if you would wait for me before you go in to see Paul. Just want to see firsthand if there's any reaction from him."

That's fine," Jo said. "I'll see you in a little while. Bye!"

Jo told Sally about the call.

"Wonder what he's thinking about?" Sally pondered. "Can you think of anything that might be upsetting him?"

"There's nothing...at least nothing that I know about. And Paul's not a private person. We talk about everything. He's never had nightmares. I'd know if he had."

"Know what I think? I think he's probably dreaming about the accident. Imagine reliving that over and over again. It must have been terrifying. Poor thing. I'll bet that's what it is."

"Makes sense," Jo sighed. "I'll suggest it to Dr. Grayson. I can't think of anything else that might be worrying Paul."

"I'm on duty at one o'clock so I won't come with you, if that's okay. I'll give you a call on your mobile later to make sure you're alright."

"Yes, that's fine. You've got to rid the city of crime," Jo said with a smile. "I won't have the mobile on in the hospital, but we'll catch up with each other sometime. What time's your break? Maybe we could meet up at the greasy-spoon café. Does he do all-day breakfasts there? I might be tempted!"

"Break is when there's nothing else going on, I'm afraid. I never know when I'm going to get a few minutes' peace. We'll catch up by phone when we have a chance, and you can fill me in with all the details when I get home tomorrow morning – that's if you're up, of course!"

Jo left for the hospital at just after 10am. When she arrived at the I.C. Unit, Ellie met her. "Just grab a seat for a few minutes and I'll find Dr. Grayson."

By 11am, Jo was beginning to realise that hospital visits were getting back to normal: waiting, waiting and more waiting. At least it was comforting to think that "normal" meant that everything was under control.

Finally, Dr. Grayson came into the room, apologising for the delay.

They shook hands and Jo mumbled something about being certain he had lots of other patients to take care of as well as Paul.

They sat on opposite sides of the low coffee table. When the doctor started speaking, Jo noticed a distinctly sheepish look on his face.

"It's Jo, isn't it?" he began. "May I call you Jo?"

"Of course."

"Jo, there are a few questions I must ask you. Please don't think I am being rude or impertinent. I'm just trying to build up a picture of Paul's life. I need to know everything about him if I am to be able to treat him."

Across the table Jo squeezed her hands together in her lap, wondering what was coming next.

"I asked you to think about things that might be upsetting Paul...things that may be causing his dreams. I have to ask firstly about your marriage. Is Paul happy at home?"

"We're fine," Jo said. "In fact, we're better than fine. We're not just husband and wife, we're best friends too. I can absolutely assure you that Paul's dreams are nothing to do with our relationship."

"I'm sorry I had to ask," Dr. Grayson said. "You do understand that if there were any problems in that area, having you at his bedside at a time like this may not be the best thing."

"Understood," Jo said, "but that's definitely not the case. We're very happy together – always have been."

"I was sure that was the case, but I had to check. Now I know, I can assure you that you can play a big part in Paul's treatment. My next question might seem equally stupid to you, but again, I must ask. Does Paul have a private life – a life away from home? A part of him that you know little about? It's not uncommon. I'm not suggesting affairs. Maybe his business life or his personal finances, his hobbies, pastimes, anything at all?"

"Paul doesn't keep anything from me. We love each other and we spend every minute that we can together. He doesn't have time for a private life. Money certainly isn't a problem. Paul's parents are extremely well off, and, although Paul hates accepting their help with money, we both know that if we need it, it's there. As far as hobbies go, he loves sport, but only as a spectator. His job is his hobby. He adores acting. There really isn't anything that I can think of that could be worrying him. Paul's a very happy person."

"Good! That's out of the way then!" the doctor said with a relieved look. "I'm sorry if I embarrassed you. The problem is that we are no nearer finding out what is causing Paul's sudden panic attacks."

"Sally – that's my friend you met the other day – she had a suggestion. What if Paul's reliving the accident? That would be pretty upsetting. Terrifying, I should think."

"It's a possibility," Dr. Grayson admitted, "but I think it unlikely. Usually, the brain has a way of wiping out such memories, or tucking them away somewhere, especially in the short term. It's a kind of instinctual self-preservation. It's more likely that Paul will remember nothing about the actual accident, but we won't know for sure until we can talk to him. No, I'm pretty certain that something else is causing his nightmares. It would be helpful to know what that something is."

"If anything at all comes to mind, I'll let you know."

"In that case, let's go and see Paul," the doctor said, standing up. "I saw a distinct sign that Paul recognised your voice when you spoke to him yesterday. I said nothing because I didn't want to inhibit you – to make you feel self-conscious when you were talking to him. I'm not suggesting that Paul is taking in every word that you say – we would have seen signs of that too had it been the case – but your initial words did cause a slight reaction. I'll be very interested to see if the same thing happens now. I don't want you to worry about it. Try to be exactly the same as you were yesterday and we'll see how he reacts."

When Jo sat down beside Paul, she looked at the monitor with its rows of wavy lines pulsing from left to right. "Hello, Paul. It's Jo," she said in a quiet and tender voice.

Immediately, there was a blip in the smooth waves and then they settled again into their rhythmic rolling across the screen.

Jo turned and looked at Dr. Grayson.

The doctor smiled and nodded. Jo turned back to Paul. She gently took his hand in hers and continued talking.

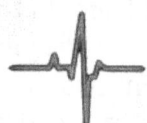

Chapter 16

When Jo left the hospital that afternoon, there were two missed calls on her mobile. One was Sally, and the other was Paul's agent, Robin Thomas.

Robin and Paul had been friends in drama school. Paul had chosen to follow a career on the boards whilst Robin had become increasingly interested in the promotional and managerial side of theatre rather than performance. He now managed several budding stars of stage and screen, as well as running a theatre company that had a growing reputation.

Several years ago, Robin had made the decision to move south, "to be closer to the action" as he put it; he now lived and worked in London. The move had meant that the two friends saw much less of each other, but the bonds were still as close as ever. When they were together, they were like a couple of school kids – always up to something, always revelling in each other's company.

Jo liked Robin. He wasn't your typical "arty - theatre" type, full of "darling" this and "darling" that. He was just a very down-to-earth nice guy. He was caring and trustworthy – a friend that Paul could rely on. Robin's name had been on the list that Jo had given to her father-in-law to contact following Paul's accident.

When Jo reached the hire-car in the hospital's car park, she sat in the driver's seat and dialled Robin's mobile.

"Hi, Robin. It's Jo – Jo Ford."

"Jo! How are you? How's Paul? I couldn't believe it when Mitch rang me. I've wanted to call before, but I knew you'd be sick and tired of explaining to people. Is he on the mend?"

Over the next few minutes, Jo filled in all the details for Robin. Her positive and confident attitude rubbed off on Paul's good friend, and the two even managed to laugh as they talked about old times and times still to come.

When the conversation got round to Paul's work, Robin told Jo that Paul had been offered the part that he had auditioned for in Scotland. "He totally wowed them!" Robin said. "But I've had to let them know the situation. Mitch told me that Paul's recovery was likely to be a long job, and, on that basis, I had to decline the offer on Paul's behalf. Pity – he was made for the role, and it would have been a huge stepping-stone for him. But don't worry, Jo. There will be other opportunities, I promise. Let's just get him back to full fitness, then we'll make him a star!"

They chatted for several more minutes, with Robin offering any help that he could and begging Jo to let him know as soon as Paul was well enough for visitors.

When Jo ended the call, she felt comforted. Robin was a real friend – the kind that Paul would certainly need. Just as Sally had turned out to be a real friend to her.

She called Sally, but her mobile was off. Jo left a message saying that everything was fine at the hospital and that she would see Sally in the morning, when she came home from her shift.

Jo stayed in town and did a bit of shopping before making her way back to her own house to park the hire-car. She went inside just to check that everything was okay.

The lamp on the living room table was still on. Jo managed a smile to herself. She was beginning to accept the fact that the broken picture and the smashed lamp bulb had, indeed, just been coincidences that her state of mind had turned into something far more sinister.

She went upstairs to grab a few more clothes to take round to Sally's. When she entered the bedroom, she placed her handbag on the dressing table and then turned towards the double bed. Jo was certain she had made the bed before leaving the house to go to Sally's, and yet the bedclothes on the left of the bed appeared disturbed.

"You're imagining things again," she told herself, as she went to straighten the duvet.

As Jo lifted the corner of the duvet, she noticed a dusty mark on the white pillow. She tried to brush it off without success.

With expectation and fear, she folded back the duvet.

As she revealed the bed sheet, she jumped backwards and tossed the duvet to the floor as if it were on fire. Her hands came to her cheeks, a stifled scream in her throat. Covering almost the full length of the clean white bed sheet was a dull grey stain. Unable to move from the spot, Jo gaped at the ugly stain. She looked at her hand – the one she had used to try to brush the dusty mark from the pillow – there was nothing to see. In sheer terror, she watched, knowing exactly what was going to happen. Slowly, oh so agonisingly slowly, the grey stain faded.

"This isn't happening! It's not real, it's in my mind. It's a shadow – a trick of light!"

She dashed to the window and moved the curtains, watching to see if, by doing so, she had made any difference in the mark on the sheets. The stain was still there – ever fainter – but definitely still there.

Just a few seconds more, and it was gone.

Jo moved back to the left-hand side of the bed. Hardly daring to touch, she reached out a hand towards the sheet. It was icy cold. She snatched her hand away.

Her mobile phone rang out. She fumbled amongst the debris inside her bag and looked at the phone's screen. It was Sally.

"Hi, Jo. I've got a few minutes, so I though I'd call.... Hello? Hello, Jo? Can you hear me? Are you okay?"

Jo tried to say yes but soon changed her answer to no. She told Sally what had happened.

"Stay right where you are – I'm on my way," Sally said as calmly as she could. "I'll be there in less than five minutes. Hold on, Jo; just keep calm."

Jo heard the police car siren and went downstairs to open the door for Sally.

"Sorry about the dramatic approach," Sally said as she grabbed hold of Jo to hug her. "Just wanted to get here as quickly as possible. Come on, come and sit down. I'll put the kettle on."

"There's no milk," Jo said weakly.

Sally turned to her partner, whom Jo had not even noticed. "Be a love and pop to the shop for some milk," she said.

Sally sat next to Jo on the sofa with a comforting arm around her shoulders.

"What's happening, Sal?" Jo whispered. "I was feeling so good about everything – so positive – and then...." Jo started to cry.

"Hey, come on now, its okay. You're safe. Paul's okay. We'll get to the bottom of this, I promise."

"Am I going mad? I did see it, Sally – I really did see it. It wasn't a trick of the light. It was there and then it was gone. I can't have imagined it all."

The two sat in silence for a few moments, neither knowing exactly what to say.

"Look, Jo, I'm no doctor and I think a doctor is what you need. You're not going mad, but you are going through an enormous amount of mental strain. I haven't got any easy answers for you. I know that you saw what you saw, but I can't explain why. Let me make an appointment for you with your G.P. Or maybe we should have a word with Dr. Grayson at the hospital."

"Not Dr. Grayson," Jo said. "I don't want him thinking I'm not up to being with Paul. I'll talk to my own doctor, I promise. But not right now, please, Sal. Just give me a little while to try to get my head straight."

"Okay! But I'm going to nag you. You have to talk to a doctor and tell them what you're going through. We can't have this happening over and over again. I'm sure that a doctor will understand and be able to help, even if it's only by telling you that this kind of reaction is quite common. Please, Jo, don't just let things rumble on."

Jo promised to make an appointment in the morning. Sally's partner returned with the milk. After coffee, Sally took Jo back to her house.

"I do have to go back to work," Sally told her, "but I'll call you when I can. Why don't you try to have a sleep? If I'm passing, I'll pop in and check on you, but I can't promise."

"Please don't worry," Jo said. "I'll just have a lazy evening and an early night. I'm fine now - honestly."

When Sally left, Jo turned on the television and sat down.

"You're fine," she told herself. "You're absolutely fine." But she knew that she wasn't.

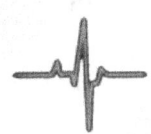

Chapter 17

Paul was a placid man. He hated violence – there was no aggression in his nature. When faced with confrontation, his policy was to walk away. He was rational to the point of being annoying at times. He was impossible to argue with. In fact, he had not been involved in anything that could be described as a fight since boyhood playground skirmishes at school.

But the smirking grin on the black Audi driver's face as he stood outside the motorway restaurant window was too much, even for Paul. This had to be sorted – and it had to be sorted now.

Paul raised a fist and mouthed a volley of abuse through the window.

The man just stood his ground and continued with his silly smile.

Paul pushed the chair away from his table with such force that it clattered to the floor. The coffee-soaked map and morning paper were left on the table as Paul rushed out of the restaurant to wipe the silly grin from the smirking face.

He reached the double swinging doors at the building's exit, pushed rudely past a young couple who was entering, and turned right along the outside wall of the restaurant, expecting to see the Audi driver waiting for him.

No one was there.

His eyes scanned the car park, searching for a black Audi. The services area was still quiet at this hour of the morning. He could see clearly that the car was not there.

"The wash rooms! That's where he'll be. There's nowhere else he would have had time to hide."

Paul entered the men's room. The area for hand basins and hand dryers was empty. He walked slowly round the corner to the urinals. No one! He looked along the long line of cubicles. The doors were all open, or at least ajar. One by one, Paul moved along the row, pushing each door fully open as he went, just to be sure. The whole room was empty.

Back outside the building, Paul scanned the area for other possible hiding places. There was no chance that the man could have reached his car and driven off before Paul got outside. He had to be somewhere...or he had to be a ghost!

When he returned to the table in the restaurant, his map and morning paper were gone and the spilled coffee had been cleaned up. Paul didn't even bother to ask – he just turned and went outside again.

As he sat in his car, his head was spinning. He didn't know why he felt like crying, but he had to rub away the tears that were forming in his eyes.

"Bastard!" he shouted, and crashed both palms against the steering wheel in a show of total frustration.

It took him several minutes to regain some composure. In an attempt to return to his normal, rational self, he began talking out loud.

"Think, Paul. Just calm down and go through everything that has happened, step by step. There has to be a sensible explanation."

Time stood still as Paul went over the hours that had passed since that black Audi Coupe had first entered his life. No matter how he tried to rationalise each and every moment, there were things that he simply could not understand. He had questions that needed to be answered, and answered now!

It was after 8am. He had two choices: ring Jo or go back to The Chair. Ringing Jo and trying to explain the inexplicable was pointless. No - let her sleep a little longer. –Instead, he would retrace his steps and confirm what he thought was fact. Maybe then all the rest would fall into place. He switched on the ignition and drove out of Hilton Park Services with a sense of purpose.

Hilton Park only services southbound traffic, so Paul had to head south to the next motorway exit before he could turn north again and try to find the pub where he had spent the previous evening. Traffic was much heavier now. Even though it was Saturday, the morning rush hour was well under way. It took nearly an hour to travel just the few miles to where Paul could see the scene of the accident on the far carriageway. The police cars were still in attendance. As he "stop-started" past, he tried to see the black car that had argued with the tree, but the heavy traffic made it impossible for him to get a clear view.

He passed Junction 12 and decided that, even though the next exit should be the one for The Chair, he would keep driving north until he reached Junction 14. From there he would turn south again and try to visualise his dramatic exit from the motorway the night before.

By the time he reached Junction 14 and turned south, traffic was thinning. After a few miles Paul saw the signs for Junction 13. This was it. He felt a sudden chill – but was it a chill of excitement or fear?

All of a sudden, Paul didn't want to know. Shaking, he slowed the car and pulled onto the hard shoulder of the motorway and stopped.

What if the map was right? What if there was no T-junction...no left turning to Rydon...no Chair? What then?

He stared blankly through the windscreen of the car, trying to come to terms with the possibility, even the probability, that the map was telling the truth.

"Ring Jo," he told himself. "Talk to her. Tell her what's happened. She'll make sense of it. Better still – just go home and forget it. Say nothing. Just make sure that you never in your life exit the M6 motorway at southbound Junction 13."

Cursing himself for being such a coward, Paul joined the southbound traffic again and drove straight past the junction. He forced himself not to look as he passed the accident scene a few miles further on. He was going home and he would put this particular Friday night and Saturday morning out of his mind forever.

He glanced in his rear-view mirror. The sight of a black car approaching to overtake him made his heart leap until he realised it was not an Audi Coupe. It would be a while before he got over this thing with black cars.

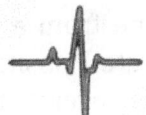

Chapter 18

The response to the appeal for witnesses to the accident on the M6 motorway southbound on Friday night had been good.

Though many drivers reported seeing the incident, most of them were driving north on the other carriageway and simply knew that an incident had occurred.

The best report came from a lorry driver. He was also driving north, but his elevated position in the seat of his cab gave him a better view of the accident. Even so, he could not be sure what had caused the crash. He reported that the black car was overtaking the white car and seemed to suddenly loose control, diving left and straight in front of the vehicle on its left.

He tried to watch in his wing mirrors as the two cars careened towards the crash barriers, but he was past the accident almost before it had happened. The cars were travelling at high speeds. His conclusion was that the black car had suffered a front nearside puncture or some other mechanical failure.

He had not called the emergency services because he was sure that vehicles travelling south would stop and call the incident in.

The chief investigating officer decided that he had now received all of the relevant information he was likely to get. He had the report from the officers who handle the accident scene. The forensic reports on the two vehicles had revealed little or nothing that the police hadn't already surmised. The eyewitness reports were helpful, but not conclusive. All the evidence pointed to the black Audi being the cause of the crash; mechanical failure had probably sent the vehicle out of control. Though it was obvious that both of the vehicles had been speeding, there would be little reason to pursue any criminal charges. With one driver dead and the other critically injured in hospital, his best course of action was to wind the police proceedings up and move on to the next case. If the insurance companies wanted to contest blame, they would both be able to see his report and make their own conclusions.

He closed the file and placed it in his "out" tray.

On his way out of the station, he stopped to ask the desk sergeant to call the scrap yard where the vehicles had been taken. "Tell them that we've finished with the two Audis. They can do what they like with them, so long as they get permission from the two insurers – they know who to contact."

As far as the police were concerned, that was it – another dead body, another case closed.

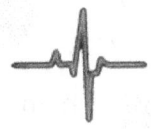

Chapter 19

When Jo telephoned her G.P. for an appointment, she was given a slot that afternoon at 2.30pm. She thanked the receptionist, replaced the receiver, and looked across the kitchen at Sally. "Two-thirty today. You happy now?"

Sally didn't take offence, but simply said that it was the sensible thing to do. "I'll probably be up before you go, but just in case – good luck! Tell him everything, Jo. Don't go leaving bits out because you feel they're silly. I'm sure he'll be able to put your mind at rest and give you something to settle your nerves."

"I probably won't see you. I'll be going to see Paul in a little while, and I'll go straight to the doctor from the hospital."

"Okay. I'll give you a call when I've got a minute and I'll see you tomorrow morning for breakfast. Guess I'm not being too much help to you – sleeping all day and working all night. I'm off from Friday 'til Monday, so we can spend some time over the weekend."

"You've been a massive help, Sal. I'd have been in bits without you. Sorry if I sounded grumpy. I know you're right. Sleep tight – and don't worry."

With that, Sally took herself off to bed.

Jo tidied the kitchen and checked to see what shopping they needed before setting out for the hospital.

She chatted to the nurses, who told her that the night had been uneventful. Both Dr.Portman and Dr. Grayson had been in to see Paul already that morning, and were quite satisfied with what they had seen.

Jo carried her plastic cup of hospital tea into Paul's room and sat down at his bedside.

She watched the monitor carefully as she said hello and, sure enough, the wavy lines gave a tiny jump at the sound of her voice. It was comforting to know that he recognised her presence. Jo wondered whether it was just her voice that had the effect on

Paul or if the blip on the monitor occurred each time someone spoke to him.

"I must ask the nurses," she told herself.

She stayed with Paul all morning, chatting away as if he could hear and understand every word. At around noon, she told the nurses that she was leaving to have some lunch before going to see her own doctor and that she would be back tomorrow morning.

She had plenty of time to go back to Sally's for lunch, but instead she decided on a visit to the "greasy spoon" for a bacon sandwich and a big mug of coffee. An hour later she was praising herself for making such a wise choice.

With an hour to spare, she drove to the supermarket and picked up the bits of shopping she had listed. She picked out a nice bunch of flowers, a bottle of wine, and a tasteful thank-you card for Sally. She had told Paul how bad she was feeling for having been grumpy with her new friend. She hoped that the flowers and the wine would make up for it.

Shopping done, she loaded the bags into the back of the hire car and set off to the doctor's surgery. Arriving ten minutes early for her 2.30pm appointment, she was surprised to be called straight into his room.

"Hello, Mrs Ford," her doctor said, "I'm so sorry to hear about your husband's accident. How are you bearing up?"

Jo was tempted to say that she was fine and just needed something to help her sleep, but she decided to do what Sally had asked and tell all.

Her doctor listened intently, making a note here and there and asking an occasional question. Jo told him of her night of terror on the bathroom floor, of the broken picture and the broken lamp. She went into detail on the strange grey stains that she had noticed on the living room floor and on the bedclothes. "They *were* there – I'm certain," she said. "Nobody else could see them, but they were there!" She found her emotions rising and had to search for a tissue in her handbag.

When she finished, the doctor looked at her and smiled reassuringly. "Shock has many ways of manifesting itself, Mrs Ford. Nothing that you have told me surprises me in the least, and none of your experiences give me any great cause for concern. Let's consider these 'grey stains' that seem to have upset you so much. I believe that you saw exactly what you say you saw. You're obviously not just making it up, and I don't think that anything I say – or anything that anyone else might say – can change the fact that those 'grey stains' were very real in your eyes. In time, you may find that you begin to question their reality. But at this moment, the unthinkable has happened to Paul and that fact tends to make the impossible seem absolutely possible in your mind. As I said, shock can be displayed in many ways.

"I also think that your friendly policewoman sounds like a very sensible person and a very good friend. Right now, you need a friend much more than you need a doctor. Don't be afraid to lean on Sally – it was Sally, wasn't it? Talk to her. Tell her how you're feeling and listen to her. Share your fears and your concerns. Don't try to hide your emotions. Just be open with her. It will help if you do.

"I'm loathe to give you much in the way of medication. I will give you some tablets to help you sleep, but I ask you to use them only if really necessary. Time will heal your problems – time and the full recovery of your husband. You were right to come and see me. I hope I have been able to set your mind at rest. You're not ill, Mrs Ford; you have suffered a terrible shock and, quite honestly, I think you are dealing with it admirably. Why don't you make an appointment to pop in and see me in a week or so? I'd like to see how you're getting on and I'd like to hear how Paul is doing too."

He scribbled a prescription note and handed it to Jo.

"Thank you, Doctor. I will come and see you next week so long as I'm not wasting your time."

"Look forward to seeing you – and you take care of yourself. Call me anytime if there is anything that you want to talk to me about."

Just as Sally had promised, Jo left the surgery feeling reassured and headed for home.

Jo decided to park at her house and carry the shopping round the corner to Sally's. As she was lifting the bags from the back of the car, a man's voice said, "Excuse me. Are you Jo Ford?"

She turned to see a smartly dressed man standing at the foot of her driveway looking rather embarrassed.

"Can I help you?" Jo said.

The man moved closer and held out his hand.

"I'm Bryn - Bryn Owen, I'm a sort of friend of Paul's. We met in Glasgow at an audition last Friday and kind of hit it off."

Jo shook his outstretched hand.

"I was so sorry to hear about Paul's accident. How is he?"

Jo explained that Paul was still very ill and had not, as yet, regained consciousness, but that the doctors were happy with his progress and he was expected to make a full recovery. She knew that the last part of her answer was still "wishful thinking," but she believed in her heart that he would come back to her in one piece. Telling others that reinforced her belief.

Bryn saw the bags of shopping and offered to help carry them to the house. Jo told him that she was taking it all round the corner to her friend's house and that she would be grateful of a helping hand.

"It's funny," Bryn said as they walked, "Paul and I were auditioning for the same part - that's not usually the basis for an immediate friendship. But we promised to keep in touch no matter what the outcome of the audition. Paul was going to introduce me to his agent."

"Robin's a nice guy," Jo said, "He and Paul have been friends since drama school. I'm sure Paul will take you to see him when he's up and about again. By the way, how did you come to hear of Paul's accident?"

"I got a call from the theatre company. To start with I was told that Paul had been offered the part and I had been chosen as his understudy - quite a result when you think of how many had auditioned. I was chuffed for both of us, and it meant that we would be seeing each other again. On Monday, they called me again and told me that Paul had been hurt in an accident, and they offered me the part. I accepted, of course, but I wish the circumstances could have been different. I managed to talk them into giving me Paul's address and here I am!"

They reached Sally's house and stood at the gate. "I'd invite you in for a coffee," Jo said, "but it's not my house. I hope you understand."

"Of course," Bryn smiled. "I just wanted to find out how things were going with Paul and to see if there was anything that I could do. I'd like to visit him when he's well enough. I popped a card through your front door with my number on. Perhaps you'll give me a call from time to time and let me know how he is."

"It was so kind of you to call. I will keep you up to date with his progress and I'm sure he'll be delighted to see you. Please don't feel bad about getting the part because of Paul's misfortune. Every cloud has a silver lining, and all that stuff. Paul will want you to make a great success of it, I'm sure. Have you got our number, in case you want to call?"

"Paul did give me his card, but I mislaid it."

Jo felt in her handbag and handed Bryn one of Paul's business cards that she always carried with her. The two shook hands again and Bryn turned to leave. He had only gone a few paces when Jo called out, "Bryn, what's the play called? Paul never told me. He said it might bring him luck and he'd tell me when he got the part."

"Oh, it's fantastic," Bryn called back. "First effort by a new writer. We're all very excited. It's quite a spooky piece. It's called *The Chair.*"

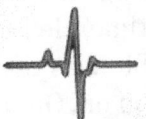

Chapter 20

Paul arrived home at around 10.30am. To his surprise, Jo was out. Saturday mornings were sacrosanct to Jo. They meant lying in bed until mid morning and then lazing around the house drinking coffee until lunchtime. He looked for a note. Beside the phone on the telephone table was the little pad that was always there to scribble information on. On the pad was written "Rydon - The Chair – Lancaster" and underneath were the usual doodles that Jo always made when she was talking on the phone.

He found no other messages from Jo, which he thought to be very out of character. He tried her mobile, but it was switched off. "No point in leaving a message – she never checks them anyhow!" he thought.

He showered and shaved and felt much the better for it. Under the shower, Paul had an idea. He would search the southbound junctions of the M6 Motorway using Google Earth – the magical programme that lets you take a wander through streets anywhere in the world, through the lens of a camera. He made coffee and took it to the spare bedroom where the P.C. lived.

When Paul turned on the monitor, he was faced with a map of Lancaster and the surrounding area. Jo must have been looking for him. Though slightly concerned, he concluded that she must have been bored and had maybe decided to have a look at The Chair herself – just for something to do.

He scoured the map in front of him. The Lancaster turning from the M6 Motorway showed no road junctions leading to Rydon – or anywhere that sounded similar.

Paul cast his mind back to everything that had happened since he had left Glasgow the day before. The drive south had been uneventful. He had stopped at the Teebay Services for coffee. Paul had travelled to Scotland many times, often as a performer in the Edinburgh Fringe. Teebay was always a favourite "coffee stop." There were northbound and southbound services, the food was good, and it was a beautiful part of the country. It was also about halfway between his home and his destination.

Paul was sure that the incident with the pillock in the black Audi Coupe had happened south of the Teebay Services. Somewhere, between there and Stafford, there had to be the turning off the motorway that led to The Chair.

He began his search.

An hour later, he had come up with nothing. Something was nagging at his brain – something to do with The Chair. That name meant something else to him, but he couldn't remember what it was. He tried to come up with all known references in his head: a fence in the Grand National; America's method of capital punishment was affectionately called "The Chair"; the chairman of a company was known as the chair. None of it made any sense.

He seemed to have completely lost several hours of his life. He had vivid memories of being in a place that didn't exist. And then there was the man who disappeared. The man with the silly grin – what was he all about?

His best hope – his only hope – was that Jo could help him make sense of it all.

It was early afternoon. Where *was* Jo? He tried her mobile again. Still switched off. This time, though he knew it was futile, he left a message. "Jo, I'm home. Where are you? I'm slightly worried. Call me when you get the message. Love you!"

The longer he waited the more worried and frustrated he became. The map of Lancaster on the computer suddenly became more sinister. Had Jo really been looking for him just for something to do? Had she needed him for something? No – she could have got him on his mobile. Had she been checking up on him for some reason? Why was she looking at that map?

He thought of ringing his parents to see if they had any ideas where Jo might be. She wouldn't have gone over to see them – he had the car. To get to them by public transport was a nightmare. But she might have told them something that would throw some light on her disappearance. He picked up the phone to call and then replaced it. "Don't be stupid," he told himself. "She's a grown woman. She's only been away for a few hours. She's probably out shopping or getting her hair done. Get a grip of yourself. She'll be back soon."

But Jo wasn't back soon.

Paul sat in front of the television watching Saturday afternoon sport. Just before 5pm, the football results started coming in. Wolves – his beloved Wolves – had lost again but so had Villa, and that made the pill a little easier to swallow.

He turned the television off and began pacing the living room, checking the front window to see if she was coming down the street, and then pacing some more. The phone rang. He leapt to answer it. No one there. He dialled 1471 to get the last caller number. "You were called today at 5.15. The caller withheld their number," an automated voice told him. As he replaced the receiver, he heard the front door open.

He ran to the hall to greet Jo. The look that she gave him could have frozen mercury.

"Jo, what's wrong? Where have you been?"

Jo pushed past him and headed for the kitchen. "Don't you think I should be asking you that question?" she snapped.

Dumbstruck, Paul followed her into the kitchen.

Jo turned to face him. He had never seen such anger in her eyes. "You've got one chance, Paul – one chance to tell me the truth. No stories, no play-acting, the truth! Where were you last night? What's her name? How long has this been going on? You can start now!"

"Jo," Paul said, holding his arms out and pleading for mercy. "Jo, I don't know what you're talking about."

"Fine!" Jo replied sarcastically. "Chance gone. I want you to pack a bag and get out! I don't want you anywhere near me. What a stupid bitch I've been. I've suspected for some time now, but I thought better of you. Go on. Pack your bag and go!"

"Jo, at least tell me what's brought all this on. You know where I was last night – or at least where I think I was. Jo, there's something very strange that has happened to me, something that I don't understand. Something that—"

"Don't bother, Paul. Even your very best performance won't fool me. At midnight, your mum phoned me. Dad had been taken ill. Oh, don't worry, he's fine, just something he ate. I've been over there all day. I tried to call you last night. Your mobile was off so I searched for your fictitious pub, The Chair, near Rydon. In the Lancaster area, you said. I even called the Lancaster Police to ask them where it was, but as you well know, it doesn't exist. So now, I don't even want to know where you were or whom you were with. I just want you to leave."

"This is crazy, Jo. There' no one else. I could never do that to you. I don't know what happened last night. I'm so confused. Please believe me. I need you to help me sort this out."

"Too late, Paul. I gave you a chance to tell the truth. Now I just want you out of here. We'll talk, but only when you're ready to come clean. Right now, I've got nothing else to say to you. Goodbye!" She pushed past him again and went into the living room, slamming the door behind her.

Paul was left standing, trying to make sense of what had just happened to his life.

"God alone knows what's going on in that man's head!" Kathy said to herself as she straightened the covers on Paul's bed. She had been watching the monitor. The tracer lines were still bouncing.

The Chair

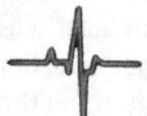

Chapter 21

Over the next few days, Jo established a routine – visiting Paul in the mornings and spending a few hours in school in the afternoons, getting ready to return full time the following week.

The doctors had told her that Paul was progressing, though apart from the removal of some of his facial dressings, Jo could see little difference in her husband. Some of the swelling around his eyes had gone down and he was beginning to look a little more like his old self, but he was still unconscious and hooked up to a whole array of electronic gadgets.

The doctors decided that Paul would be given until the beginning of the following week before he would be woken from his slumbers. Dr Portman would have liked to give him more time to recover from his physical injuries, but Dr Grayson had persuaded him that Paul's mental situation needed to be investigated sooner rather than later. The neurologist was still concerned about the amount and intensity of Paul's brain activity.

Paul's parents had visited on several occasions, usually in the afternoons so that someone from the family was with Paul most of the time. Jo had received countless "get-well-soon" cards and messages – many from people she didn't even know. Funny how people only get in touch when there's a disaster.

Sally had been a rock to Jo. Their friendship had blossomed and there had been no mention of Jo returning to her own house. Sooner or later, she would have to make the move back home, but for the time being, she was settled and happy living with Sally.

On Friday, when school had finished, she sat and talked with her headmaster. He wanted to be sure she was ready to come back on Monday morning to take on her full class work again.

"You only have to say if you need more time," he had told her.

But Jo was adamant that getting back to normality would do her good, and she could do little for Paul until he was taken out of his coma. When that happened, she told the headmaster, she would find out from his doctors how important it would be for her to spend time with him, and then she would talk to him again.

On leaving school she called in at her house just to check that everything was okay and to pick up any mail. As she was leaving, a car pulled up outside her gates. It turned out to be the policeman who had headed the enquiry into Paul's accident. After the obligatory "So sorry" and "How he getting on?" and "How are you feeling," the policeman asked her a few questions, none of which she was able to give much of an answer to. He told her that as far as the police were concerned the file was closed. "It was just a dreadful accident, Mrs Ford. It's impossible to level blame and, even if we could, there would be little point in us pursuing things. It wouldn't help Paul or you."

Jo confirmed that she was happy to accept that the accident was indeed just a terrible accident, and that all she wanted was for Paul to be able to recover and try to forget. She was pleased to hear that he would not have to face police questioning.

"I'm not saying that we won't want to talk to him once he *is* fully recovered," the policeman added, "but it will be more a case of him helping us to understand what happened rather than anything else. I promise you that we won't do anything to hinder his full recovery."

The policeman left and Jo headed round the corner to Sally's house.

Thirty miles away at Bob's Breakers, a car-breakers yard in Stafford, Bob Cummings was making a few phone calls. Audi Coupes were not common in scrap-yards and to have two of the things fall into your lap at the same time presented a chance to make money that was too good to miss. Both the police and the insurance companies had given him the okay to do whatever he liked with the two cars. What he liked was making money!

Bob was ringing round a few friends and colleagues to let them know that the Audis were there, if there were any bits they needed. Even in the crumpled state the cars had arrived in, Bob was sure there was plenty of profit to be made from them.

"Mike!" he shouted to his yardman. "I want those two Audis put somewhere easy to get at. We'll be having punters looking at them over the next few days. Make sure they're safe to work on, will you?"

Mike was new to the scrap-car business. All he could see were two smashed remains of what used to be posh motors. "Okay, boss, but I doubt that there'll be much that we can sell from those two."

Bob smiled to himself. He knew better than that. With the cost of spares being what it was, there would be plenty of interest in salvaging everything possible from those two beauties. Without thinking, he found himself rubbing his hands together.

Outside in the yard, Mike started up the forklift truck to move the Audis into a space just beside the two main entrance gates.

He had moved the white car and was about to drive the forks of his truck through the side window spaces of the black Audi when he had the distinct feeling that he was being watched. He spun his head round to look out the back of the cab. There was a man standing across the yard smiling at him.

"Won't be a minute," Mike shouted. "Just got to move this one and I'll be with you."

He turned back to concentrate on locating the forks into the Audi. The car had vanished!

Not believing his eyes, he jumped from the cab and looked around.

The smiling man was nowhere to be seen. When Mike's eyes reached the main gates, his mouth dropped open.

There, lying alongside the white Audi was the black car – exactly where he had intended to place it.

"Well done!" said a voice behind him. It was Bob.

"You ain't gonna believe this, boss, but *I* only moved the white one – the black one moved of its own accord!"

"Yeah, Mike, that'll be right. Parked itself perfectly too, I see! Have you been on the happy juice again? Come on; let's get these gates closed. I've had enough for one day."

"No – honestly, boss. I was about to pick it up when I saw this guy on the far side of the yard. I told him I'd be with him as soon as I'd moved the motor and when I turned round, it had moved itself."

"So where's the guy now?" Bob asked.

"He disappeared."

"Wow - disappearing customers as well as wrecks that move themselves – you have had an exciting day!"

"Boss, I'm telling you—"

"I don't know what you're on, Mike, but it must be bloody good stuff! Now come on – help me with these gates. Time to go home."

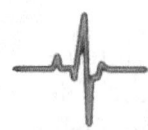

Chapter 22

It didn't take Paul long to realise that he shouldn't be driving. Two close shaves – one at a junction, where he hadn't noticed an approaching car and had pulled out straight in front of it, and another when the car in front of him braked and Paul nearly ended up in the back of it – told him to find somewhere to park and leave the car.

In any case, he had no idea where he was going. His mind in a daze, he was just driving aimlessly.

He pulled onto the car park of The Dog and Gun, his local pub. Paul had no intention of going inside. He wasn't a drinking man, so he had no thoughts of finding the answers to his problems at the bottom of a bottle.

Instead he once again tried to relive the trip home from Scotland. There must be something he was missing, but he could only remember the black Audi, the race, and The Chair. Anger, confusion, frustration, and fear were joined by hurt now. How could Jo believe that he would abandon her for another woman? Why wasn't she with him right now, when he needed her most? It wasn't long before another emotion joined the list: desolation. His whole world had fallen to pieces. He was broken.

Where do you go when you finally hit rock bottom? Where do you go for help when you are helpless? Where do you go to find hope when everything looks hopeless?

You go HOME!

Paul reached for his mobile and dialled his parents.

He knew what to expect. Jo had been with his parents and would, without any doubt, have told them of the situation. They would have heard that their son had been unfaithful. Mitch and Grace were "parents" to Jo too and, in the same way that he was running to them for help, Jo would do exactly the same.

The truth was that he had done nothing wrong. But was that the truth? He wasn't sure of anything anymore. His mum answered the call.

"Mum, it's Paul."

In a concerned but loving tone, she asked where he was and if he was okay.

"I'm fine. How's Dad?"

"Complaining a lot and being a general pain in the backside! He's fine – don't worry about him."

"Mum, I know what Jo will have told you. I can't explain over the phone. What I do want you to know is that she's 100% wrong. I don't blame her for thinking what she's thinking, but I swear to you, Mum, there's never been anyone else in my life since I met Jo and I hope there never will be."

"That's all I needed to hear," Grace said. "Come home. We need to sit down with your Dad and talk this through. We love you both, Paul – you know that. You don't have to say anything else right now. Just come home. It doesn't matter how late it gets - We'll be waiting up for you."

"Thanks, Mum! I'm on my way."

"You drive carefully. I hate to think what your state of mind is like. Please take care!"

"See you in about an hour. Don't worry - I'll be careful."

When Paul arrived at his parents' home, it was obvious that the story Jo had told them had been a devastating blow to both his mother and his father. Both had been adamant that they couldn't believe it and they had tried their best to convince Jo that there must be a reasonable explanation to Paul's "missing" night.

"Jo's a stubborn girl," his father said. "She was hurting so much. She obviously wasn't thinking straight. Nothing we could say seemed to make any difference. She loves you so much, Paul. Jo just feels dreadfully let down – but we'll sort this out. Grace, dear, why don't you give Jo a quick call and let her know that Paul is with us?"

"No!" Paul interrupted. "You shouldn't call her. I know Jo. It won't do any good – in fact, it may have the opposite effect. She will feel that you're taking sides. She'll feel isolated. I need you both but so does Jo – she hasn't got her own parents to turn to. Please don't call her. Not yet."

Mitch, Grace, and Paul sat around the table in the spacious kitchen and talked.

By the time Paul had recounted his last twenty-four hours, it was past midnight. Mitch and Grace had listened intently to all that Paul had told them. From time to time, they asked questions, but for the most part, they just let Paul talk.

Paul had tried his best to tell his story without emotion. He still didn't understand what had happened, but by telling the whole story quietly and calmly he at least began to realise how it must sound to his listeners. When he had finished there was a short silence before the questions started.

"So you think that The Chair must have been just a dream?"

"What about the man at the motorway services? Was that part of the dream or did you really stop there and buy a map?"

"If this was a dream, when did you wake up? When did reality begin again?"

Paul tried his best to field all of the questions but his answers just seemed to create more uncertainties. Paul just didn't know what was fact and what was fiction, and no amount of talking was going to help unravel a very confused mind.

The more they talked, the more frustrated and angry Paul became.

Eventually, Mitch said, "I have an idea. I know a doctor – I play golf with him. He's very 'into' the use of hypnosis. What we have established tonight is that, for some reason, your mind has become dreadfully confused. Maybe *he* can help. The truth about last night has to be somewhere in your brain. Perhaps *he* could bring it out. I've only ever seen stage hypnotists at work and, to be honest, I've always thought of their acts as bit of a sham, but he obviously finds the method very useful. What do you think? Is it worth a try?"

"Anything is worth a try," Paul said. "I have absolutely nothing to hide. I've told you the truth – or, at least, the truth as I recall it. I'll do anything to put my life back together. Yes! Bring him on. Let's give it a try."

"Sunday tomorrow," Mitch said, "I would have been at the golf course but for this damn food poisoning. He'll be there. Why don't you drive me over and we'll catch a word with him – see if he thinks he can help."

"If you're sure you feel well enough to go," Paul replied enthusiastically. "I have to get this sorted out. I can't spend day after day not knowing what's going on in my head."

"That's settled then. Grace, make another cup of tea, love, and then we should all get some sleep."

The monitor screen showed nothing but smooth wavy lines. Paul was relaxed. His mind was at ease. The nurses went about their routines. Everything was good.

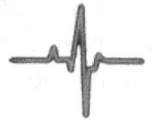

Chapter 23

Sunday morning was always a busy time at Bob's Breakers. D.I.Y. car enthusiasts used their weekends to indulge their hobby. Half the fun was doing things as cheaply as you could, rummaging around scrap-yards and modifying bits of motors that shouldn't really "fit" to save spending megabucks on the manufacturers' recommended parts.

Sunday was "Mon-ey-day" to Bob Cummings. Monday was his day off.

"Mike!" Bob shouted into the yard. "Take a look at the rear-exhaust sections on those two Audis, will you? I've got a punter arriving in about half an hour. He just needs the bit including the back box. I noticed that the black car had a fancy chrome extension pipe fitted. Take a look at that one first. If it's not too badly damaged, start taking it off, will you?"

"Will do, boss." Mike grabbed his toolbox and headed for the Audis.

The black car was lying on its roof, wheels pointing skywards, the full exhaust system clearly visible. The force of the impact against a solid tree had buckled the whole chassis of the Audi Coupe. There was a distinct kink in the exhaust system, but the main damage appeared to be nearer the front of the car where a bracket had torn loose and the pipe had split. The rear section, including the shiny chrome extension pipe, looked good. Mike surveyed the fitting points and reached in his toolbox for the necessary spanner.

Kneeling at the side of the car, he began dismantling. He fitted the spanner socket over the first nut and then reached toward the exhaust pipe to give himself extra purchase to turn the handle.

The moment that his left hand connected with the pipe, he tumbled backwards in shock and pain. The exhaust was red-hot. His flesh was burning.

He got to his feet clutching his injured hand between his knees.

His screams of abuse were heard all the way to the office where Bob was pouring coffee.

"Christ! What's he done now?" Bob muttered as he made his way outside.

Mike was kneeling by the side of the Audi. A man was standing at the entrance to the yard, smiling.

Bob rushed over to Mike and knelt beside him. "What have you done?" he asked, noticing that Mike was clutching his hand. "What's happened?" he shouted, raising his head towards the man at the gates. The man had gone.

Bob's attention returned to his yardman.

"Bloody exhaust's red hot!" Mike screamed. "Look at my bloody hand!"

He held his injured left hand out for Bob to see.

Apart from being slightly cleaner than usual, the hand appeared to be normal – no sign of burns.

"You bloody great ninny!" Bob laughed. "There's nothing wrong with your hand. Scared the life out of me, you idiot. What's your game, anyhow?"

Mike seemed to come to his senses. He looked at his hand and flexed his fingers. He stood up, backing away from the black Audi as if it were about to attack him.

"It's that bloody car, boss. I'm not going anywhere near the thing. I'm telling you – the exhaust was red-hot when I took hold of it. Why would I make it up? I told you yesterday that it had moved itself. The bloody thing's alive. I'm staying away from it!"

Bob could see that Mike was seriously upset. Making fun right now was not the thing to do. "Come and have a coffee – I've just poured it," he said, putting an arm round Mike's shoulders and leading him towards the office. "I'll get the exhaust off while you calm down a bit. By the way, who was the guy by the gates? Were you dealing with him? He's gone now."

"What guy? There was no one else in the yard."

"Not to worry," Bob said. "Get a cup of hot coffee down your neck and I'll go and work on the Audi. That punter will be here soon."

A couple of minutes later Bob came back into the office with a frown on his face. "What the hell have you done to the chrome extension on that exhaust? It's just a dull grey now. Did you try to wipe it with a greasy cloth or something? I'll have to get some polish out and clean it up again."

"I never touched the bloody extension pipe. It was still bright and shiny when I looked at it."

"Well it ain't bright and shiny now! Come and have a look."

The two men walked over to the black car. The chrome exhaust extension was anything but bright and shiny and yet, as they watched, the haze on the metal began to clear. In less than a minute, the chrome was sparkling again.

"Told you!" Mike exclaimed. "That bloody car's alive. I'm not working on it. You can bloody sack me if you like."

"And why would I want to sack you?" Bob smiled, putting a hand on Mike's shoulder. "Think how incredibly boring my life would be without you and your fantasies. Now bugger off and get some work done before I change my mind. Go and sort those tyres out. We're bound to have plenty of punters looking for part worns today. Pick out the best ones and put them on one side."

Mike turned and walked away.

"In wheel size order!" Bob shouted after him. When Mike had gone, Bob picked up the spanner that lay on the ground where Mike had dropped it. He glanced over his shoulder, just to make sure that Mike was out of sight, and then, very gingerly, he touched the exhaust pipe of the black Audi.

Stone cold.

In a matter of minutes the exhaust was off the Audi, cleaned up and ready for sale.

As they were closing the gates that night, Mike said, "So how do you explain that chrome extension pipe cleaning itself before our very eyes then, boss?"

"Act of God," Bob laughed. "The good Lord just wants me to make money, and who am I to disappoint him? Act of God, my son. Forget it. Now, if you talk to him nicely, perhaps he'll sort all those tyres out before Tuesday morning, because you made a right pig's ear of it!"

The two men went their separate ways – Bob to his home, Mike to the pub – both of them thinking about the "act of God" and both of them knowing that there was more to it than that.

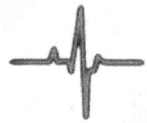

Chapter 24

Paul and his dad arrived at the golf course early. Paul had driven them there in his dad's Jag. At least the car didn't look out of place in a car park that was filling quickly with Rollers and Bentleys and other hideously expensive rides.

As the two men rounded the corner of the clubhouse, they were hit by a view straight out of a glossy advertising brochure.

The course stretched as far as the eye could see. A thin white mist was still clinging to the manicured fairways that sparkled with dew in the early sunlight. Autumn had ambushed the surrounding woodlands and the array of colours was stunning. Paul could not help but stop for a moment to absorb the beauty that was all around him.

Mitch had gone a few paces ahead and was chatting to a group of men that were heading off to start their rounds.

As Paul caught up with his father, Mitch was wishing them luck and the caddy cars began moving towards the first tee.

Mitch put an arm around his son's shoulders and raised his other arm, gesturing towards the scene that Paul had been admiring. "That, my son," he said, "is probably the best reason in the world for playing golf. Isn't that just breathtaking?"

"It's magnificent," Paul replied. "It's just such a shame that the game doesn't live up to the thrill of the venue."

"Philistine!" Mitch grunted, giving his boy a quick smack on the back of his head. "One day you'll realise that sport isn't all about kicking lumps out of your opponents and then pretending to be mortally wounded when things aren't going your way."

They turned and headed towards the suitably imposing club house, a converted Victorian mansion house that had been added to over the years but had managed to maintain its period style perfectly.

Inside, Mitch led Paul to a huge lounge dotted with comfortable chairs and low coffee tables. "Grab a seat," he said.

"I'm just going to have a word with the starter to find out what time Martin is playing. Back in a minute."

Paul stood and watched his father disappear through a long hallway. In the lounge, Paul chose a burgundy leather armchair close to the open double doors.

Mitch was soon back with the news that Martin was teeing off at 10.30am. "He'll be here long before then," Mitch said. "Martin wouldn't miss his coffee and bacon rolls before his Sunday morning exertions."

"Exertions!" Paul snorted. "Dad, this is a round of golf were talking about. Didn't someone once call it 'a good walk spoiled'?"

"Sometimes I wonder where I went wrong bringing you up," his dad laughed. "Anyhow, talking of coffee and bacon rolls, what do you say to sampling the delights of our humble clubhouse kitchen? And before you start, 'humble' *was* a joke!"

"Sounds good to me, but are you sure you should be eating bacon rolls? I thought you were on a strict diet after your visit to the hospital."

"There are some pleasures that I simply refuse to give up - one of which is Mrs B's bacon rolls. Stop worrying about me. I feel much better today, and I'll limit myself to just one - but don't tell your mum!"

Mitch got up and left the lounge in pursuit of breakfast.

Since they had arrived at the golf club, Paul had noticed that everyone who saw Mitch wanted to say hello and have few words. His father was obviously well liked and respected in this haughty environment that boasted money and influence everywhere he looked.

He was proud of his dad, and rightly so. Mitch had not been born into money. He made his vast fortunes by sheer hard work and determination. He was the first to admit that the lucky breaks had always come his way at just the right moment, but the truth was that he had built his businesses with shrewdness and skill. More importantly, he had done it all with loyalty and truthfulness and honesty and compassion. Wealth had not made him cynical or unreachable; it had made him generous and grateful. Yes, Paul *was* proud of his "old man" - and rightly so!

Mitch returned and about ten minutes later a stout woman in a white apron approached their table carrying a tray of coffee and a mountain of bacon rolls. He stood and, gesturing at Paul, said, "Mrs B, this is my son Paul. Paul, Mrs B, the second best cook in the world. I have to say that because your mum comes here sometimes and I wouldn't want anyone 'grassing' on me!"

Mrs B put the tray on the coffee table and offered a hand to Paul. "He's a silver-tongued old devil," she grinned. "Nice to meet you, Paul."

Paul shook her hand. "And you, too," he said standing up. "Now I can see where his waistline comes from!"

"Waistlines are nothing more than a number on a measuring tape," Mitch retorted.

"That may be so," the cook said, resting her hands on her ample stomach, "but both you and me could do with making those numbers a whole lot smaller, Mr Ford!"

"And just how am I supposed to do that with a temptress like you around?" Mitch asked.

"Temptress, am I? Sure I'm just a simple girl trying to earn an honest crust." She said with an Irish lilt. "Enjoy your wicked pleasures, you two! Glad to see you're back to your old self, Mr Ford. We were worried yesterday when we heard you'd been in hospital."

"Thank you, Mrs B," Mitch said tucking paper money into the pocket of the white apron. "We certainly will enjoy!"

"Thank *you*, Mr Ford. Lovely to have met you, Paul."

With that, she turned and left and the two men started demolishing the mountain.

Half way through their breakfast, a tall silver-haired man in a bright pink sweater and equally loud large-check trousers approached. Mitch turned his head and immediately jumped to his feet. "Martin!" he said holding out his hand, "come and join us. You're just in time to rescue us from certain coronary failure. Come and help us finish Mrs B's bacon rolls. Sit yourself down - I'll get another coffee cup. This is my son Paul."

Martin pulled up another chair and began tucking in to the remains of the mountain.

Mitch reappeared with a clean cup and poured more coffee for them all.

"The starter told me you were here and wanted to talk," Martin said. "Is this business or social?"

"Bit of both, I suppose," Mitch replied. "I wanted to ask your advice and maybe a favour."

Twenty minutes later, Paul and Mitch had explained the situation.

When they finished speaking, Martin was quiet for a moment, obviously deep in thought.

Finally, he looked straight at Paul.

"The first thing to say is try not to worry. What you are experiencing, although personally very disturbing, is actually quite common. As you so rightly say, the truth about those lost hours will be somewhere inside your head. The mind has a habit of locking things away that it considers...undesirable. Whether hypnosis is the answer to unlocking those secrets quite frankly depends on you. Different people react very differently to hypnosis. If you turn out to be receptive of the process, then I may be able to help. If not, there are other avenues to explore. I'll be happy to help if I can."

He paused and looked at his watch.

"I can imagine how desperate you are to find some answers. I'm due on the first tee in about ten minutes, but this afternoon was just earmarked for tidying up the garden and that can wait. Why don't you come over to my place at around 3pm?

We can carry on this chat then, and I'll see what I can do – but no promises that we'll get a result."

"That's so kind of you," Paul said, "I'll be there. Thank you so much!"

"Thanks, Martin," Mitch added. "You're a good friend."

Martin stood up to leave.

Mitch shook his hand again. As Martin walked away, Mitch said, "You'll send the bill to me."

Without turning his head, Martin waved a hand in the air and replied, "I've already been paid in full. Those bacon rolls are worth their weight in gold!"

On the drive home Paul said what a lovely man Martin appeared to be. Mitch told him how the two had become friends many years ago. Martin had lost his first wife to cancer and the experience had all but broken him. He had become something of a recluse. Mitch met him when Martin had been offering the fishing rights to a lake on his property for sale. Mitch had always liked a bit of fishing and had gone to see Martin and the lake. The two men had instantly bonded and over the next few years, Mitch had been able to coax Martin back to a normal life. He had introduced Martin to the woman who eventually became his second wife.

"I think he feels indebted to me, though there is no reason why he should. He has more than repaid any kindness that I might have shown. There have been plenty of times when I needed a friend to talk to –things your mum could not have helped with. Martin's always been there for me. He's a very clever doctor. Much respected. I have every faith in him."

Back at home, Paul and Mitch passed the rest of the morning wandering in the garden, checking the greenhouse plants and generally enjoying the fine autumn weather.

They ate a light lunch Grace prepared and read the papers until it was time for Paul to go and see Martin.

"Come with me, Dad. I want you to be there. Whatever comes out, I want you to hear it firsthand. I need you to be absolutely sure that I'm telling the truth. Jo thinks the world of you. She trusts you implicitly. I'm going to need you to help me convince her that I haven't cheated on her. Please, Dad, will you come?"

"Of course I'll come, but not because I have any doubt that you're telling the truth. And be sure of this, Paul: whatever we may find out about those lost hours, we'll handle it."

Grace wished them luck and they set off to unravel the mystery of Paul's drive home from Scotland.

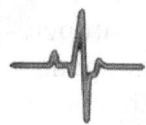

Chapter 25

Sally and Jo had spent a relatively quiet Saturday. Jo visited Paul in the morning and did some shopping before getting back to Sally's in the mid afternoon. Sally had just lazed around doing bits of housework and enjoying her break from the pressures of policing.

There was a decent movie on television that night that both of them wanted to watch, so they decided to order in a pizza and slum it.

The movie turned out to be almost moderate, which perfectly complimented the pizza. They did manage to watch it through to the bitter end, but that was due to sheer determination rather than any sense of enjoyment. As the end titles scrolled up the screen, Jo heaved a sigh of disappointment.

"Can't win 'em all, I suppose. That's the worst Johnny Depp movie I've ever seen. I'm still trying to work out what was going on. Did you get any of it?"

"Only the bedroom scenes, my dear, only the bedroom bits. I certainly got those."

"Mmm! He is dishy. Couldn't you just—"

"Stop right there, Mrs Ford. You're a married woman – and in answer to your question, yes, I could. But that's okay, 'cause I'm a single girl."

On the television, the trailer for a new cookery show caught Sally's attention. "Must put that on to record," she said. "I love those kind of programmes just for all the little tips you pick up."

The conversation turned to food. They chatted about personal likes and hates and found that their tastes were very similar. Both liked Italian food and could enjoy Indian, so long as it wasn't too spicy. Chinese food was a no-no, French was okay but often too fancy for its own good. When it came to the top of the culinary pops, there was no doubt that good old traditional English dishes were the overwhelming winners.

At around 11.30, Jo said that she was going to bed. "What's happening tomorrow?" she yawned. "Anything special?"

"Only if you call my birthday special," Sally replied in a nonchalant tone.

"You cow!" Jo shrieked. "Why didn't you tell me?"

"Thought you had too many other things on your mind. Anyhow, I'm past the age where you want to advertise that another year has slipped by."

"All the same, we must do something to mark the occasion," Jo insisted. "What about your mates down at the station? Surely they will be planning something?"

"I dread to think what!" Sally groaned. "We'll probably have a drink on Monday after the shift. But tomorrow my diary is empty."

"Then let's fill it." Jo sat down again and looked at her friend. "You absolute horror! I can't believe that you didn't tell me. Never mind! What would be your perfect day? Excluding bedroom romps with Johnny Depp!"

"If Johnny's not available, I suppose that Plan A would be that you visit Paul in the morning as usual, I have a lie-in until at least mid-day, and then I come and meet you at the hospital and you treat me to a slap-up Sunday dinner at a not-too-expensive restaurant that I know. How does that sound?"

"Sounds good to me. What's Plan B?"

"That's a little trickier," Sally said, pretending to be in deep thought. "Plan B is that you visit Paul as usual, I have a lie-in until mid-day, then I come and meet you at the hospital and you treat me to fifteen courses at the Dragon Palace on the High Street."

"But that's Chinese," Jo protested. "Neither of us like Chinese!"

"So I guess that's a no to Plan B!" Sally grinned. "Looks like were stuck with Plan A."

"That's settled then," Jo said, standing up and making for the living room door. "One o'clock at the hospital. I'll meet you by the front reception desk – and don't go dressing up, 'cause I'll just be casual and I don't want you showing me up!"

"It's a date," Sally replied, "and thanks, Jo!"

As Jo was leaving the room, she turned and looked back at Sally. "You know what, Sal? You are totally mad! Barking! Insane! You're a policewoman, for God's sake! A pillar of society. We look to people like you to protect us and help us and what do we find? We find that you're as mad as a box of frogs! I despair!"

"Night, Jo – I love you, too. Sleep tight!"

Jo was still muttering in tones loud enough to be heard as she climbed the stairs to bed. "Absolutely bonkers...off her rocker...definitely not the full shilling...radio rental...a sandwich short of a picnic."

Sally just snuggled up with her favourite cushion and smiled to herself. "It's a funny old world!" she whispered to herself.

Jo woke early the following morning. She showered and dressed and, even before making coffee, walked to the petrol station at the end of the road, where she bought a bunch of flowers and the rudest birthday card she could find for Sally.

Back at the house, she found a suitable vase and left the flowers standing in water, still wrapped in their cellophane. Sally could have the fun of arranging them. She left the card propped up against the vase.

She made coffee and toast, quickly dismissing the fleeting thought of taking Sally breakfast on a tray. Even though she had only known her friend for a few days, Jo knew that to disturb Sally's lie-in would be bordering on sacrilege.

At just before nine, she walked round to get the hire car, and drove to the hospital.

In I.C. Unit 3, all was calm and quiet. Ellie was on duty and reported that Paul had enjoyed a mostly peaceful night. As was usual, he had shown moments of disturbed mental activity, but everyone was used to that by now; jagged lines on his monitor screen no longer caused the same level of concern.

Jo sat with him and talked. She had found that talking about the news and sport and the weather for hours on end was impossible, and so she had begun reading to him. She had chosen a favourite story of his, a book that he had owned since childhood: *Three Men in a Boat* by Jerome. K. Jerome. If ever Paul were to own a dog, it would surely be named Montmorency.

Strangely, time seemed to fly by when Jo was with Paul. It would have been understandable if such a one-sided conversation appeared to slow down the clock, but for some reason, Jo found the opposite to be true. She became totally lost in this new world of tubes and wires and boxes of electronics and a body that she so wanted to hug. Paul would wake up. She was sure. Paul would wake up and he would be his old self again and she would know that she had done her duty as a loving wife and been at his side "in sickness and in health."

Just before one o'clock, Jo made her way to the reception area at the front of the hospital to look for Sally. Her friend was already there, waiting for her.

"How's the patient?" Sally enquired.

Jo told her that all was well.

"Thanks for the flowers and the card. No one else buys me flowers. They're beautiful!"

"You'll have to get out more," Jo laughed. "We're going to have to find a Johnny Depp substitute for you as quickly as possible."

"My life's complicated enough without having men around," Sally replied.

"Ah, but think of the benefits Sal. They do have their uses," Jo gave a knowing wink.

"Enough of this line of conversation. Are we ready to execute the rest of Plan A? I'm starving!"

—╱╲—

Sunday lunch was delicious: roast beef and all the trimmings, followed by hot apple pie with lashings of thick, calorie rich cream, coffee, and chocolate mints.

"Good plan!" Jo said, when they had finally finished all they could eat. "I am totally stuffed. What about you?"

"Reckon I could still go for one of those sticky toffee puddings that were on the sweet trolley," Sally lied.

"Glutton! Do that and we'll need the trolley to get you out of here!"

The two were still laughing when Jo's mobile rang.

She fumbled in the depths of her handbag and eventually answered the call.

—╱╲—

"Hello, Jo. It's Ellie."

Jo knew immediately from the nurse's tone that something was wrong.

"Is Paul okay?"

"There's been a bit of an unexpected change. Don't worry. Everything is under control. I thought it best to let you know in case you wanted to come back in."

"What's happened?" Jo asked, panicking.

"It's hard to explain over the phone. We're not 100% sure what's going on, but Paul is being looked after and you mustn't worry. Are you able to come?"

"I'm just around the corner, as it happens," Jo said. "I'll be with you in ten minutes. He is going to be okay, isn't he?"

"I'm sure he'll be fine. We'll fill you in when you get here. Just keep calm. See you in a few minutes."

Sally had watched as Jo's smile dropped and a look of terror replaced the laughter of a few moments ago. "What's up, Jo?"

Standing and gathering her things together, Jo explained the telephone call.

"You go," Sally said. "I'll get the bill and follow you round. Try to stay calm until you know what's going on. I'll be with you as quickly as I can. Off you go!"

Outside, Jo flagged a passing taxi. It would be quicker than walking to the car.

Less than ten minutes later she was opening the double doors to I.C. Unit 3, petrified of what she might find inside.

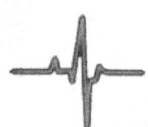

Chapter 26

Paul and Mitch arrived at Martin's house at 2.45pm.

The unremarkable frontage disguised the luxury that was within.

Mitch noticed Paul's amazement at the surroundings. "Not short of a bob or two, these doctors," he joked. "Wait 'til you see the grounds. The lake that I was telling you about is bigger than my whole place. You wouldn't think it when you come down the front drive, would you?"

Martin's man servant/butler had opened the door to them and was leading them towards some large glass doors at the end of an expansive hallway.

"It's stunning," Paul said. "Is it just Martin and his wife who live here?"

"Just Martin and Gilly and Gerald, the butler. It's quite a place. There have been a few changes since Gilly arrived on the scene. Needs a woman's touch, a place like this! It was going to rack and ruin when I first met Martin."

Once through the glass doors they were met by Martin, who shook both their hands. "Welcome to the humble abode." he smiled, almost apologetically.

It was one of those moments when Paul knew that there must be a suitable reply but the words simply wouldn't come.

"Take a seat, both of you. Gerald will be making tea. He does so as a matter of course, whether I ask for it or not."

"Sounds perfect to me," Mitch said. "How did the golf go? Are you still robbing unsuspecting members of their twenty quids?"

"I played okay for a duffer," Martin grinned. "As a matter of fact, I did take the money this morning – much to the captain's annoyance!"

"You're a bandit, Martin. The handicapper will catch up with you one of these days. Maybe then I'll get some of my hard-earned cash back."

Paul had left his seat and was standing at the French windows, looking out over Martin's domain.

"Fancy a stroll?" Martin asked. "Feel free to wander, if you wish. I guess that us two old 'uns will just wait for the tea."

"No," Paul said, "but it is beautiful. When you said that you were only going to be 'tidying the garden,' I just imagined a few flower beds. This is immense."

"You should have seen it before Mitch introduced me to my wife. It was more like the Amazon rainforest. They say that wild boar roamed free out there!"

Paul laughed. "Well it's certainly a magnificent sight now. I'll bet it takes some effort keeping it looking like that."

After tea and more small talk, it was time to get down to business.

Once again, Martin tried to explain the vagaries of hypnosis. "All we can do is try and see what we find."

He led them to another room that was kitted out with all sorts of expensive-looking equipment. There were several simple hard-backed chairs and a doctor's couch.

"Jump up on the bed," Martin said to Paul. "I'm going to hook a few wires up to your head. Don't worry, there's no pain involved. It's just so that I can keep an eye on what's going on electronically whilst I have you under my magic spell."

Paul obliged and was soon connected to Martin's gadgets.

"Here's the plan," Martin said, "Once you're under I'm going to try, firstly, to regress your mind to your childhood – just to get an indication of how receptive you might be to this process. Then we'll move forward, maybe to your early twenties and find out what you were doing then – so if you've got any dark secrets, speak now."

Paul shrugged and shook his head.

"Finally, we'll try to bring you right up to date and see if we can get you driving home from Scotland. That might be the trickiest bit." Turning to Mitch, he said, "Grab a seat. This will take a little while, so make yourself comfortable." Looking again at Paul, he asked, "Are you ready to start?"

"Ready when you are, Martin."

"At the top of the wall in front of you is a small black spot. Do you see it?"

"Yes."

"I want you to concentrate on that spot and nothing else. You will hear me talking, but that's not important. All that matters is the spot on the wall."

Martin continues to talk in a very calm flat tone. In what seemed like just a matter of seconds, he turned to Mitch and said, "That's it, he's sleeping. We can talk freely."

"That's amazing. I don't think that I'll ever be comfortable talking to you again. Now I know how you always beat me at cards!"

Martin smiled. "It's not always that easy. Paul may be a good candidate for this. Let's see, shall we?"

Over the following minutes, Paul was taken back to early childhood. Mitch acknowledged when he remembered some of the things that Paul was remembering. He listened to his son, often with tears in his eyes.

Martin pointed to one of his gadgets. "See the lines moving across that screen? Those display the electrical pulses from Paul's brain. They give us an indication whether he's calm or upset, happy or angry. Those smooth wavy lines that you see right now show contentment. Paul was happy with his childhood."

The process continued with Paul moving on to drama-school days and his early times with Jo.

Finally, Martin tried to bring him forward again – to Scotland and his audition and to the journey back home.

The session continued to go well. Paul seemed very happy. The audition for *The Chair* had been fantastic. He had given it his best shot. Things began to change when Martin prompted him to see the black Audi Coupe that was approaching from behind.

"Where are you now, Paul?"

"Stoke - just passed the exit for Stoke, What on earth is this idiot doing? What are you smiling at, you tosser? Piss off! I've had enough of this – time to lose you, you bloody moron!"

The smooth, wavy lines had turned into a range of sharp mountain peaks. Then, in an instant, the monitor flat-lined. Nothing! No electrical input. Paul's brain had shut down.

"What's happening?" Mitch demanded in a worried voice. "Get him back, Martin, for Christ's sake – get him back!"

"Calm down, Mitch. He's sleeping, look at his breathing. He's not experiencing any panic or discomfort. We must leave him for a few minutes. He's hit a mental block – something his brain refuses to remember. Something pretty drastic, I'd guess. Give him a couple of minutes to see if he can come out the other side. If not, I'll wake him, but the chances are that we'll have to go through all of this again if we ever want to find out the truth."

Five minutes passed and the lines on the monitor hadn't moved.

"I'm counting down from ten, Paul. You can wake up when you're ready."

Paul's eyes opened. He looked at Martin and Mitch. "Good God! You two look terrible! Whatever have I been saying?"

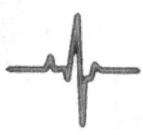

Chapter 27

Inside I.C. Unit 3, Jo's first contact was with Ellie.

"Come and sit down for a minute," Ellie said, ushering Jo towards the waiting room. "Would you like a drink? I'll get someone to bring tea."

"No...no, thanks! What's happened Ellie? Is it bad?"

"I'm probably not the right person to answer that question, Jo. In fact, at this particular moment, I'm not sure anyone could answer that question. I'll try to explain. Physically, Paul's condition hasn't changed. He's still recovering well, as far as we can tell. The change has been in his brain activity. Ever since day one, Paul has had periods of excessive activity in his brain – periods when he appeared to be mentally stressed, maybe angry, maybe frightened. We can't tell. It was those periods of stress that led the doctors to put Paul into his state of induced coma. About an hour ago, the opposite happened to Paul. Instead of his brain showing excessive activity, it ceased to show any activity at all."

"You mean he died?" Jo butted in, terror in her eyes.

"No, Jo," Ellie went on, "he didn't die. His heart rate and breathing remained constant and strong. Paul is very much alive. The decision that we faced was, how long could we risk leaving Paul in what was potentially, a critical state? That decision fell into the lap of Dr Patel, who I don't think you've met. Both Portman and Grayson were off duty – even consultants get have days off. Dr Patel decided that the risk of doing nothing was greater than that of bringing Paul out of his coma, and so we began the process of waking Paul up."

"Is he awake now? Can I see him?"

"We are giving Paul drugs that will wake him very gradually – it's a process that will take many hours. The strange thing was that, not long after the decision was made to wake Paul, his brain began functioning normally again. If we'd waited, we would probably have left him in his coma. But once we had started to administer the drugs it may have been dangerous to try to reverse the process."

"So when do you expect him to wake up?"

"It's likely to be early tomorrow morning. Dr Portman is on his way to the hospital now, and he will be here with Paul when his eyes open. Dr Grayson is also being contacted and we fully expect that he will be here too."

"Can I be here? Can I wait? Maybe he'll need me. I want to stay!"

"Of course you can stay, Jo. No one's going to send you away from Paul, but it will be a very long and boring wait. I suggest that you hang on until Dr Portman gets here and have a chat with him. He will know exactly what the procedure will be when Paul finally wakes up. He can let you know how soon you will be able to see your husband. Talk to him, Jo, and take his advice."

"Yes. Yes, I'll do that, Ellie. Can I see him now?"

"I'm afraid it's a bit like Piccadilly Circus in there at the moment," Ellie told her. "Different bits of equipment are being taken in and out. There are other things that we need to keep an eye on, now that the waking process is underway. It's probably best if you can just wait a while until Dr Portman comes in. Then we'll see. Now, how about that cup of tea?"

"That would be nice," Jo said.

As Ellie stood up to leave, Jo felt a hand on her shoulder. She hadn't noticed that Sally had come into the room whilst she and Ellie were talking.

"Hi, Sally," she said. "How much of that did you catch?"

"I got the gist of it," Sally said, taking the chair beside Jo and squeezing her hand. "Maybe it's a good thing that they're waking Paul up now. I know how frightening this must be for you, but it's a moment that had to come sometime. Once Paul is awake, the doctors will be able to find out so much more. They won't have to guess anymore. They'll know what to do, and they'll do it. You've been so brave, Jo, so wonderfully positive, all along. Don't falter now. "It's going to be okay – that's what you've been telling me ever since we met. Now I'm telling you: It's going to be okay. Paul's going to wake up and he's going to be fine."

Try as she might, Jo could hold back her tears no longer. Sally hugged her and tried to comfort her but she knew that nothing she could say or do would be much help. At a moment like this, words were simply inadequate.

By the time Dr Portman arrived at the unit, Jo was calmer. Sally had stayed with her, and they had concentrated on all of the positives of the situation.

"Why don't you pop off now? "Jo suggested to Sally. "It's your birthday, for heaven's sake! You shouldn't be sitting in a hospital waiting room. You should be out partying."

"I'd much rather party with you tomorrow night," Sally replied, trying her best to keep the positive vibes going. "Let's just wait and see what Dr Portman has to say. I'd sooner be with you!"

When the doctor came in, his face immediately told Jo and Sally that everything was under control and going well.

"Hello, Jo. Hello, Sally," he smiled. "That husband of yours has given everybody a bit of a scare, Jo!"

"Have you seen him?" Jo asked, even as she realized how stupid she must have sounded.

"I've seen Paul, I've talked to the rest of the team, and I totally agree with the decisions that were made. If I had been here, exactly the same would have been done. So, this is where we are. Paul will wake sometime early tomorrow. Until then, apart from us keeping a very close eye on him, there is little that any of us can do. Jo, there is a room you can have if you want to stay – that goes without saying. But I'm afraid it's a very small single room; I don't really have anywhere that I can offer to you,

Sally. It's coming up to seven o'clock now. It's going to be a very long wait and I would be happier if you didn't wait alone, Jo. Please, go home where you can be comfortable and have Sally's company. I promise you that I will call you the moment that Paul wakes up – whatever hour of the morning that might be. What do you say?"

Jo thought for a moment and looked at Sally.

"Come home," Sally said. "It really does make much more sense than waiting here. We can be back at the hospital within a few minutes of the doctor's phone call. I'll come with you. I'll bunk off work. Come on, let's go home."

"You will let me know if anything else happens in the meantime?" Jo asked Dr Portman.

"You know I will. Listen – just over a week ago, Paul somehow survived an accident that would have been the end for most of us. Frankly, I was amazed at how little *real* damage he had suffered when I saw the state he was in. Paul has been very lucky so far. I have a good feeling that his luck is going to continue. Tomorrow, all being well, we will begin planning his full recovery. You know that there are no promises in what I say, Jo, but it is honestly what I believe. Go home, get some sleep, and let's see what tomorrow brings."

"Thank you, David," Jo said, not realising that she had used his Christian name. "I really am very grateful for all that you are doing."

"See you tomorrow," Dr Portman said, shaking Jo's hand. "Get some rest. It's going to be a long day."

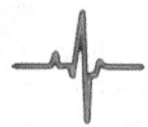

Chapter 28

Martin smiled at Paul. "Don't worry, you haven't given any secrets away, and you haven't shocked your Dad too much!"

"Did you find anything out? Paul asked, expectantly.

"Before we talk about that," Martin asked, "what's the title of the play that you auditioned for in Glasgow?"

"It's called *The Chair*," Paul said. As soon as the words came out, his eyes widened and his mouth dropped open. "How in God's name did I fail to make that association?" Paul gasped. "How could I possibly have come up with this story of the pub and not realised that I had given it the same name as the play? I bet Jo made the link. No wonder she thinks I'm lying! You must think I'm lying, too." He looked at Martin and his father.

"No, Paul, you're not lying," Martin said. "You're just a little confused. It seems pretty clear that the pub and all that happened there is just fantasy – a dream, if you like. The reality is your trip to Scotland, your audition, the journey home, the black Audi Coupe – but there we meet a problem. When you were describing your journey to us, I introduced the black car into your thoughts. Not long after that, we hit a total mental block – your mind went completely blank. You flat-lined on my screen up there." Martin pointed to the screen and the waves that were rolling rhythmically across it. "Something happened that your mind has tried to erase, but we still don't know what that something is. What we do know is that *that something* is the truth."

"So where do we go from here?" Paul asked.

"I think it unlikely that hypnosis alone is going to do the trick. Whatever the truth is, you are going to have to relive it, so that your brain can process it and accept it. I'd like you to talk to a colleague of mine – he's what Americans call a 'shrink,' though I know he hates the term. He's a good guy. We've worked closely on many cases, and often with great success."

"Fine!" Paul said, looking at his father. This sounded expensive, and he knew Dad would be getting the bill. "When could this happen?"

"Bob lives and works down in London, so you'll have to go down there to see him. I'll call him tomorrow and see when he can fit you in. He won't keep you waiting if he knows that you're a personal friend of mine. Is there any day next week that wouldn't suit?"

"Any time, any day will be fine with me," Paul said. "My life isn't going anywhere until this is sorted out."

"Quite! I do understand, and I'm sorry that I've not been more help to you. I'll ring Bob and let you know what he says."

He disconnected Paul from his machines and the three men took a brief walk in the gardens of Martin's home before leaving. Mitch thanked his friend and Paul promised to try a round of golf with Martin and Mitch "one day soon."

As they were walking towards the Jaguar in Martin's drive, Martin called to them from the porch, where he was standing.

"One thing you could try," he said to Paul. "Take a drive up the M6 past the Stoke turnoff and then turn back towards home - relive that bit of the motorway. It might just bring back something."

"I've already done that," Paul answered. "I did it yesterday morning, before I went home. I was looking for the turning to the pub."

"Do it again," Martin insisted, "but this time, do it at night – at about the same time that you would have been driving on Friday night. Things are different now. Your brain knows that the pub thing is all a fantasy, so that all goes out of the equation. I'm not saying that it will work, but it's worth trying."

"Don't worry," Mitch said, "I'll go with him and make sure he does what you say."

"No, Mitch!" Martin said. "Paul has to be alone in this. Anyhow, he wouldn't want you chirping in his ear – it would spoil the drive!"

"Understood," Mitch called back, laughing. "Thanks, Martin. You're a good friend."

At around 8pm that evening, Paul set out to retrace his Friday-night journey down the M6 motorway. He had planned a route that would take him north, almost as far as Warrington using "A" roads rather than motorway. Just south of Warrington, he would join the M6 southbound and head back for the Midlands.

He had chosen to drive as far north as Warrington so that he could spend some time on the faster motorway, and let his mind become acclimatised, before reaching the stretch near Stoke, where he hoped that something would happen to help him understand the disaster that the last forty-eight hours had been.

The night was cold but clear. "A" roads demanded a greater level of concentration than motorway driving, but even so, Paul found his mind wandering, desperately trying to find a scrap of information, a split second of memory, that might help him find the answer to his lost hours.

He knew now that the pub called The Chair was just fantasy. What he didn't know was where fantasy began or, more importantly, where it ended. Was his stop at the Hilton Mains service area part of the fantasy or was it reality? Surely it had to be part of the fantasy because that episode of the story also contained the mystery man from the black Audi. But how *could* he be sure? If Hilton Mains was fantasy, where did the reality in his life begin again? Was all of this just a bad dream? Had Jo really kicked him out? His head just went round and round.

A signpost told him that he was approaching Warrington. The turning for M6 southbound was on the right in one mile's time. He took the turn and a few moments later he was heading down the slip road to join the M6. A glance at his watch told him that it was nearly 10pm, the precise time that he had planned to start his journey south. He would be at the Stoke turning in about half an hour.

Though the Audi was only pleasantly warm, Paul could feel sweat forming on his forehead. He cracked open the driver's window. A chill blast of air hit is face. He found that he was constantly checking his mirrors, looking for black Audi Coupes. Traffic was light. The constant roar of the wind rushing by made him close the window again.

He was approaching the Stoke turnoff, travelling in the inside lane of the motorway at just over 70mph. As the blue and white junction sign flashed by on his left, Paul felt a sudden chill. The hairs on the back of his neck stood up. Fear gripped him.

"Hello, Paul," a soft voice said.

Looking in the rear view mirror, Paul saw a face that he knew, a face with a silly, taunting smile.

The Audi swerved violently across two lanes before Paul managed to regain control.

"Steady, Paul. Not yet! You'll end up killing both of us if you drive like that!"

"Who the hell are you?! How did you get in my car?" Paul shouted.

"You can call me Simon," the man said, "though it doesn't really matter. I don't think we're going to be friends."

"Too bloody right we're not going to be friends!" Paul screamed, trying to half concentrate on his driving.

"I've been so looking forward to this moment," the man continued. "You should be pleased to see me, Paul. It *is* the truth that you're looking for, isn't it? That's why you came out here tonight – remember? I'll tell you the truth. I'll remind you of the moment your mind is trying to obliterate – the moment you are so ashamed of."

"I'm not ashamed of anything! Who the hell are you?!" Paul demanded again.

"You disappoint me, Paul. You know very well who I am. I'm the man you killed!"

"He's having another nightmare," Kathy said. "Better get Dr Portman down here, and Grayson too, if he's arrived yet. It might be that this sort of brain activity will wake him up early. Let's get the whole team alerted. We'd best be ready for anything."

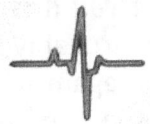

Chapter 29

"This isn't happening," Paul said calmly. "This is all in my mind."

"The funny thing about dead people," Simon said, "is that half of the time the living want to bring them back, and yet when they do come back, you either don't believe that they're real or you want to get rid of them."

"Piss off!" Paul shouted, "I've had enough of this." He tried to move the car over towards the hard shoulder of the motorway but the car didn't respond. He tried the brakes. Nothing!

"Now, Paul," Simon continued in a condescending tone, "you don't think that I'd let *you* drive this car in your present state of mind, do you? You'd probably get us both killed."

Paul tried the brakes again. The sudden realisation that he was not in control of the car, somehow made the whole situation more acceptable – utterly terrifying, but more acceptable. "What do you want?" Paul asked.

"That's better, Paul. Chill out a bit," Simon said. "I knew you'd take this in the right spirit – no pun intended!"

"Cut the crappy jokes, Simon. You were the one who wanted to race!"

"Ah! So you do remember? That's right – I was the one who wanted a race. I just wanted a bit of fun, but you took things a bit too seriously, didn't you, Paul?"

"If you managed to kill yourself, don't blame me!" Paul said. "I turned off and left you stranded. I wasn't going to race with an idiot like you."

"And you went to The Chair and stayed the night, didn't you, Paul? I saw you there."

The mention of The Chair threw Paul's mind into even greater confusion. "There is no Chair," he answered, uncertainly. "That was all a dream."

"No Paul, there is a Chair -- it's nice place too. You went there, but not exactly in the way you seem to remember."

"Let's just cut the bullshit. You seem to know everything, so you tell me what happened. I've got my fantasy – now let's hear yours."

"It's a bit cramped in the back of this coupe," Simon said. "Why don't I pop into the passenger seat where we can talk more easily?" In an instant, he was there, sitting right next to Paul. Still grinning. "That's better," he said, stretching. "Unsociable car, the Audi Coupe, but fun to drive, wouldn't you say?"

Paul ignored the question.

"What's up, Paul? Cat got your tongue? I'm sorry. This must all be a bit of a shock to you, I can see that. So let's just get to the truth that I promised you. We're almost there now - almost exactly where it all happened."

"Where what happened?" Paul demanded.

"The climax. The final scene. The "dénouement. Come on, Paul, you're an actor, this is the good bit – the bit the audience has been waiting for."

"Bollocks!" Paul sneered. "Just get on with it, will you?"

"No need to get tetchy, Paul. Just trying to appeal to your dramatic leaning. Anyhow, just about here you decided that you'd had enough of this idiot pulling alongside you and then dropping back in behind you and flashing his headlights. I don't blame you, Paul. I'd have been upset too. You decided that it was time to lose me - pedal to the metal...burn me off. I was delighted, of course; now the race was on. I let you stay in front for a while, then it was time to see what these two little Audis could really do. We'd better speed up a little bit now, Paul – just to make this more realistic."

The car suddenly surged forwards, picking up speed until the clock showed nearly 110mph.

"That's better," Simon grinned.

"What the hell are you doing?" Paul shouted as fear gripped his whole body. "Is this all about revenge?"

"Not revenge, Paul, I'd rather call it justice."

"What are you going to do, you maniac?"

"About a mile and a half further on, I decided to overtake you again. I drew alongside you and I was almost past when you chose to edge out and squeeze me up against the central reservation. That was nasty Paul – that wasn't playing the game at all. You touched the back corner of my car, spinning me out of control, right across your path. The inevitable occurred. We both left the road - through the crash barriers and into the field. My car hit a tree and I was killed instantly. You, on the other hand, cartwheeled end over end down the bank and came to rest, wheels in the air. You died, too, Paul. It's true – but only for a few moments, and then you managed to claw your life back again."

"This is insane! This never happened!"

"Don't interrupt, Paul. We're nearly there and I wouldn't want you to miss the best bit. We're going to relive the whole thing, but this time just in your car. We're going through those crash barriers again, in exactly the same place. And here's the deal, Paul: if you survive for a second time, I'll leave you alone, forever. I'll accept defeat. If you die, I'll have had my justice. How does that sound, Paul?"

"You're mad!" Paul screamed.

"No, Paul, I'm dead, remember? When you're dead, insanity isn't an option. Now, a little more speed should take us past that red car in front, just in time for our exit – stage left."

Paul watched, helpless, as the red car flashed by on his left. He noticed the woman driver's look of sheer terror as he flew past. He gripped the steering wheel hard, but it made no difference. The Audi slewed to the left at over 110mph - hit the crash barriers and went airborne into the field beyond.

In I.C. Unit 3, all eyes were on Paul's monitor. Suddenly, the crazy zigzag of lines went flat.

It was 2.30am on the day after Sally's birthday. Paul had never regained consciousness.

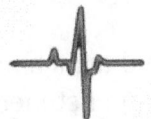

Chapter 30

The car park of The Chair was deserted.

Inside, the drinkers chatted and laughed over their pints of real ale. The restaurant was busy too, and the delicious aromas from the kitchen mingled with the sweet-smelling wood smoke from the log fire.

Paul sat in the big old armchair, next to the fireplace. He watched the flames dance and listened to the crackle of burning wood.

The man behind the bar waved to him, as if he were an old friend.

"Simon was right," he thought. "Nice place – The Chair."

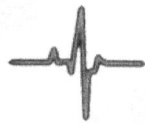

Chapter 31

Dr Grayson walked into the small office where David Portman was studying the notes in Paul's file.

"We need him to wake up, David. It's been over three hours now since we got a bleep out of his brain. Last time he flat-lined, it was only a matter of minutes. We need him awake – and soon."

"So what would you like me to do?" Dr Portman snapped. "Set off an alarm clock? You know the process. He'll wake when he's ready. Maybe you'd like to shout 'Boo!' in his ear, or something. I'm as concerned as you are, but we've done all we can. Now we just wait."

Dr Grayson held up his hands in a defensive gesture. "Take it easy, David," he said. "We're on the same side here. I was just stating a fact. I wasn't suggesting that there was anything more you could do to speed up the process."

"I guess we're all a bit jumpy with this one. There's something strange about this guy – something that I can't put a finger on. If you talk to the nurses, they'll tell you the same thing. All these nightmares that he's been having, and now the total loss of any activity in his brain – it's weird, almost spooky. Sometimes, when you're alone in the room with him, it's almost as if someone else is in there, watching. Kathy has even reported seeing someone in the corridor."

"We'll all know a hell of a lot more about our friend Paul when he finally decides to open his baby blues," Dr Grayson said with a smile. "Ten quid says that he's fine when he wakes up – no permanent damage. He'll be out of here within three weeks. Want to take the bet?"

"No bet!" David laughed. "That's exactly what I mean when I say there's something strange about this guy. Look at the state he was in when they brought him to us, and yet everyone on the team expects him to make a full recovery – mentally and physically. There isn't a single doctor or nurse in here that would take your bet. Why are we all so sure? What is it about this guy?"

Ellie poked her head round the door. "He's waking up!" she said.

Paul's return to consciousness – the moment that would indicate whether the rest of Paul's life might be compromised – turned out to be about as dramatic as a trip to the supermarket.

There had never been any doubt in Dr Portman's mind that Paul's physical recovery would be absolute. When he had finished surgery on his patient early that Saturday morning his words on leaving the theatre had been, "We've saved the body; let's pray we don't lose the mind!"

Now it appeared that those prayers might well be answered. Paul's initial responses were unbelievably normal. It was as if he had just woken up from a good night's sleep...give or take a few minor impediments.

Jo was called once Dr Grayson had made an assessment of Paul's condition, and her entrance into the room had proved to be a touching moment for everyone.

In an instant, the fears that Paul may not recognise his own wife were gone. There were tears, of course, as well as hugs and handshakes. The monitor screen showed a row of soft wavy lines. Jo would indeed have her man back in one piece.

In fact, Paul's return to the land of the living had been so "matter of fact" that everyone was delighted when he fell back asleep. For so long, they had all craved for the chance to talk to him; it seemed bizarre that they should now be happy for him to sleep again.

"Why am I not astonished?" Dr Grayson said as he relaxed with the team over coffee in the little waiting room. "In just the few short hours since waking up, he has made it abundantly clear that he is mentally okay. That amount of head trauma would have suggested a considerable amount of lasting damage, or, at the very least, a long, hard fight to regain normality. We have seen something that is almost incredible – in a way, something unnatural."

"I hope I'm not putting a damper on things," Ellie said, "but it's almost as if I'm waiting for the bomb to drop...for something to go wrong. I think that we all expected a positive outcome – though I'm not sure why we were all so confident. But this is just too good to be true. Are there any concerns that there may be a backlash somewhere along the line?"

"It's hard to be absolutely sure," Dr Grayson replied, "but everything appears to be *so* normal that I think it unlikely Paul could be fooling us all. At this moment, I think we just have to accept that Paul is a very, very lucky man. We do need to keep a close eye on him over the next few days, but I'm not anticipating a 'backlash.' as you put it, Ellie."

The next few days proved Dr Grayson's assessment to be accurate.

Jo, Sally, Mitch, and Grace visited regularly. Robin, Paul's agent, had been to see him, as had several of his "actor" friends. All were amazed and delighted at his obvious progress.

Paul went from strength to strength both physically and mentally. Physiotherapy on his injured legs was having an immediate and positive effect. His visual wounds were healing well and would leave less scarring than had first been feared. The healing of his internal injuries continued smoothly, and the damage that he had suffered would leave no lasting effects.

The one thing that continued to amaze his doctors was the fact that Paul's mind seemed to have not been compromised in any way.

The more they talked to him, the more astonishing the revelations became.

When Paul had first woken from his coma, the fact that he had seemed to know exactly where he was and exactly what was happening had come as quite a shock to his caregivers. The fact that he seemed to know whom everybody was seemed even more unlikely.

Dr Grayson could hardly believe what he was hearing when Paul told him that he had been aware of what was going on around him throughout his time in I.C. Unit 3. He had listened to Jo talking to him each day and reading to him from his favourite book. He had heard the doctors discussing his case at his bedside. He knew about Sally and about his football team's results. He knew what the weather was like and what was going on in the news, because Jo had told him. To all intents and purposes, he had been "awake" for most of the time.

How could it be that such extensive and brutal damage to the human head could result in little or no effect to mental faculties? Dr Grayson was intrigued.

During his many sessions with Paul, Dr Grayson inevitably broached the subject of the "dreams" that Paul appeared to be having during his induced coma.

Paul was able to recount everything, in precise detail, though he said that he had been too embarrassed to discuss his dreams with anyone else – not even with Jo.

He told Dr Grayson of his night at The Chair, and his journey home via the Hilton Mains services. He told how Jo had thrown him out and of his trip to his parent's home and the visit to Martin for hypnosis.

He told of his drive to Warrington and his attempt to relive his journey home that Friday night.

It was at this point only that his recollections became a little blurred. The next thing that he could clearly remember was his second visit to The Chair.

"How do you feel about knowing what actually happened on that Friday night – about the accident? About a man being killed?" Dr Grayson asked him.

"It's strange," Paul said. "I knew about the accident and the man's death all along. I heard you all talking about it, but the fact that I knew what had really happened didn't seem to make any difference to my dream. In my dream, I was searching for a truth I already knew, I guess."

"And what about the man, Paul – the man at the Hilton Park services? What do you make of him?"

"Do *you* believe in ghosts, Doctor?" was Paul's reply.

In a later conversation with Mitch and Grace during a visit to see their recovering son, Dr Grayson was able to confirm that "Martin" didn't exist. It was just another piece of the complicated puzzle that was Paul's brain.

Almost exactly one month to the day after he was admitted to I.C. Unit 3 of the Wolverhampton Royal Hospital, Paul was allowed to go home. He was still using crutches, but he would be able to dispense with them soon. His life was getting back to normal. He was indeed a very lucky man!

Chapter 32

Paul and Jo had enjoyed the Christmas and New Year celebrations with Paul's parents – celebrations that had seemed to have even more meaning this time. His parents and Jo were all aware of how close they had come to losing their beloved Paul.

Saturday, the 21st January, was a special day. It was derby day - the meeting of the Wolverhampton Wanderers and Aston Villa at Molineux stadium. Jo had treated Paul to a South Bank ticket but had decided to let him enjoy the match without worrying about her tagging along. She hated football anyhow.

Jo drove Paul into town to save him the bother of parking. They arranged a meeting point for after the match and agreed to eat out in town that night. Paul promised that he would not let the result of the game spoil their enjoyment. Win, lose, or draw, they would have a pleasant meal together and a romantic evening. He kissed his wife through the window of the Ford CMax they were driving now. He waved to her as he joined the crowds headed to the game.

The afternoon was crisp and cold but the promised snow had not arrived. Molineux Stadium looked fantastic. It was the first match that Paul had been to this season. The pitch was a perfect carpet of green. All around him were fellow Wolves supporters decked in anything that they could find, as long as it was "old gold and black." The few Villa supporters were at the other end of the ground, bravely sporting their "claret and blue" – dangerous colours to be wearing on an afternoon like this.

It was a typical derby game – plenty of effort and plenty of fierce tackles, making attractive football impossible. This was certainly not a good advertisement for "the beautiful game."

Half time came with the match still goal-less.

Several of the seats around him were temporarily vacated as their occupants joined the queues at the fast food stands for pies and hot drinks. Paul stayed put, still soaking in the atmosphere.

"Paul!" a voice shouted. "Paul – up here!"

Paul turned round in his seat to look where the voice was coming from.

Three rows behind him, topped with a gold and black pom-pom hat, Paul saw a smiling face – a smiling face he had prayed he would never see again.

"Didn't know you were a supporter," Simon shouted. "Come up here. There's a spare seat next to me."

Paul turned back and faced the pitch again, his mind frozen. He wanted to look behind, just to make sure that he'd seen what he thought that he'd seen, but fear wouldn't let him.

Instead, he stood up and made his way to the gangway between the rows of seats. He had to get out. He kept his eyes fixed firmly in front of him. As he was leaving, he heard, "See you soon, Paul. Take care now!"

Outside the stadium, Paul just walked, not caring where he was going. He heard the roar as the players emerged for the second half of the game. More by luck than judgement, he found himself walking in the direction of the Half Way House pub on Tettenhall Road – the place where he had arranged to meet Jo after the game.

He stopped at a newsagent's shop and bought a packet of cigarettes. He didn't know why – he hated smoking. When he reached the pub, he ordered a pint and a double scotch. He didn't know why – he didn't drink alcohol.

He took his drinks to a table outside the pub where he could smoke. It was freezing cold. He didn't even notice. He didn't notice when, nearly an hour later, Jo was walking towards him.

"What on earth are you doing, Paul?" she asked in a tone of utter disbelief. "You hate cigarettes. You don't drink, either. What's happened, love? Surely losing one-nil to Villa doesn't warrant this sort of reaction?"

"I'm sorry, Jo. I've had a bit of a funny turn. Can we just go home now?"

It was obvious to Jo that something serious had happened. Without any further questions, she took Paul's arm and helped him to his feet. "Come on, love, the car's just round the corner. Let's get you home. You must be freezing."

They drove home in complete silence.

When they entered the house, Paul made his way up the stairs and into the bedroom. Jo took her coat off and hung it on the hall stand, then followed him upstairs.

Paul was lying on the bed staring at the ceiling, still fully clothed, shoes still on.

Jo knelt beside him and stroked his face. "What's happened, love? Please tell me what's happened."

"Can you give me a little time?" Paul pleaded. "I know that this must be very scary for you but I'm okay. I just need a little time to think. Please don't worry. It's fine - really, it's fine!"

"You can't expect me to not be worried," Jo said, feeling the tears in her eyes. "Please don't shut me out, Paul. Talk to me."

Paul turned his face away. "I'm sorry, Jo. There's nothing I can say right now. I have to get things straight in my head. We'll talk later – I promise – but not right now. Just let me be alone for a little while."

"Shall I call the doctor?"

"No. No doctors, please. This isn't something that doctors can help with."

"Let me take your shoes off; you'll be more comfortable. You can slip under the covers and sleep."

"Just leave me. Please, Jo, just leave me alone and stop fussing!" Paul said irritably.

Jo stood up and left the room, not knowing whether hurt or worry was her uppermost emotion. When she reached the living room, she phoned Sally, but her mobile was off and she wasn't answering the house phone.

As soon as she replaced the receiver, the phone rang. "Is Paul there?" the voice said.

"He can't come to the phone at the moment. Who's calling?"

The line went dead.

Jo made her way to the kitchen, close to tears.

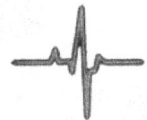

Chapter 33

When Paul appeared from the bedroom later that night, he moved close to Jo and hugged her like she'd never been hugged before.

"I'm so sorry, honey," he said, and Jo could feel that he was crying.

Jo hardly knew what to say. Something like "It's alright, Paul," struggled out, but that was all.

Finally, Paul loosened his grip of her body and took her face gently in his hands. "I know that you're looking for an explanation, but I'm not sure that anything I say will satisfy. I can't even explain things to myself. I'm going to tell you the bare bones of what's happened and I'm going to ask you to leave it at that, at least for the time being. Will you try to do that for me?"

"I don't know how to answer that," Jo whispered. "I've never seen you like this, Paul. I'm scared! Scared for you, scared for me, scared for us."

Paul seemed to think for a moment, then he spoke in a very soft, calm voice.

"For the first time since my accident, I've had what I can only describe as a flashback. I don't want to go into detail because by doing so I'll just be making myself remember things that I'd rather forget. It shook me up, Jo; it shook me up very badly. I'm sure that you can see that. I can't imagine any other way of dealing with this than by just trying to forget it. So that's what I intend to do, and I need you to help me by not asking for any more detail than I've just given you."

"There's one thing I must ask you, Paul. In your fantasy world, you dreamt that I threw you out because you were having an affair. Please tell me that this flashback has nothing to do with our relationship. If you can tell me that, I'll be satisfied."

"I swear to you what happened today was about the accident – not about us."

"Then forget it. But you must promise me one thing: if anything like this happens again, you'll go to Dr Grayson and talk to him about it. I need that promise, Paul."

"You have my word, honey, and thank you for being so incredibly understanding."

"What about food then?" Jo asked. "I'm starving, and I haven't forgiven you yet for not taking me out to dinner tonight like you promised."

"I'm starving too," Paul agreed. "And, by the way, I haven't forgiven you yet for kicking me out of my own house in my fantasy."

Jo threw her arms around his neck. "I'll never kick you out, my love, never ever. But if you even think of having an affair, I'll kill her before you get the chance to get started!"

The top layer of ice that had formed between them melted away but, underneath, Jo knew that Paul still had his demon to deal with. How soon would it be before they would go through this scene again?

$$-\!\!\!\wedge\!\!\!-$$

Half an hour later, Jo had concocted something dramatic to look at and unbelievably tasty from some chicken breast, peppers, vine tomatoes and basil.

After they had enjoyed their meal, Paul and Jo chatted long into the night.

They held a ceremony to dispose of what was left of the packet of cigarettes that Paul had bought. When the last cigarette had walked the wooden spoon plank and fallen into the waiting bowl of soapy water, Paul looked up at Jo and said something that she could hardly believe.

"Of course," he said, "there would be no question of cigarettes ever entering this house again if we had a baby!"

In an instant, tears welled in Jo's eyes. "What did you say?"

"I said that maybe we should think about trying again, but only if we both agree that we will not let failure affect our lives like it did before."

"I so want to bear your child – our child," Jo said moving around the kitchen table and hugging Paul until he nearly fell from his chair. "Let's try, Paul, please let's try again. This time will be different. This time we will know from the start that the chances may not be great; that way, failure won't seem like failure. There'll be no blame, no wondering why. If it happens, that will be fantastic; if it doesn't, we'll still have each other."

"Better get started then," Paul grinned. "After all, you're not getting any younger!"

"You cheeky pig!" Jo laughed, and the two of them went happily to bed.

In the midst of their lovemaking, Paul suddenly stopped.

"What's wrong?" Jo asked, worried.

"Nothing's wrong, love. I was just thinking that if only I could have included this in my fantasy world, I'd have been hoping for flashbacks every day!"

"Who needs fantasy when you can have the real thing?" Jo purred, encouraging him to start again.

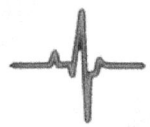

Chapter 34

For several months, Paul and Jo lived an almost normal life. Their attempts to produce a baby Ford were still proving unsuccessful, but they both kept their promise to each other that this would not affect their otherwise happy life.

Paul was working again. Robin kept him as busy as possible with small "walk-on" roles in T.V. shows, and there was always a fair share of work to be had in advertisements. Paul was a good-looking guy. The breakthrough role still eluded him though. He auditioned, unsuccessfully, for several parts, but he kept his spirits high, always believing that his time would come.

He took Jo to Glasgow to see *The Chair* with his friend Bryn Owen playing the leading role. After the play, Bryn took them to dinner and insisted they stay the night with him in his rented house. Paul had wondered how he would feel watching the play that was supposed to be his own big chance, but he thoroughly enjoyed Bryn's performance and was pleased to hear that other offers were beginning to roll in for his friend.

He had also worried about how he would feel driving home along the route that had been the scene of his accident. He talked to Jo about his feelings and, though it meant a far longer journey both in time and miles, they decided to take a completely different route home, cutting across country to Edinburgh and then taking the A1 south before turning west again for the Midlands.

What Paul hadn't told Jo was that his main concern was not the M6 motorway; it was the thought that Simon might be there, waiting for him.

The almost-normal life that Paul had been enjoying would have been perfectly normal but for the occasional incident that reminded him that his demon was still around.

Simon had not appeared again since that day at the football match, but every so often, Paul would notice something that was obviously meant to remind him that his presence was still around. There was the time that he got into his car after a visit to his parents' house. The cold night air had left the inside of the windscreen misted with condensation. There on the screen, in front of his eyes was a big letter "S." It could only have been drawn from inside the car. Then there was the photograph that he carried in his wallet, a picture of him and Jo posing beside the new white Audi Coupe. Somehow, a crease had appeared as if the photo had been folded. The line of the crease was not in the centre of the picture but it ran exactly between himself and his wife - separating them.

There were other incidents, like T.V channels changing when he was watching, a bloodstain on a favourite shirt, things moving from the places where he knew that he had left them. All of these "little" things could easily be explained away and Paul would try to dismiss each one as it happened, but deep down he knew that Simon was playing with him.

Unbeknown to Paul, Jo was also experiencing happenings. For her, the incidents were always the same: shadowy grey stains that magically faded as soon as she noticed them – on the bed, on the chairs, on the kitchen floor, even in the bath. Jo kept her findings secret, but she could not get away from them.

Spring was late arriving that year; in fact, it seemed to Paul, the seasons were less clearly defined these days. The one thing that was certain was that every season had become duller and wetter.

Paul had taken up jogging – not in a fanatical way, but he enjoyed a run. He was more conscious of his general fitness since the accident, but pounding the roads was more than just a physical exercise for Paul. The time he spent jogging was time when he could reflect on life in general and, in particular, on the antics of Simon.

On a late April evening, Paul was on one of his runs around the perimeter of Wolverhampton's West Park, a distance of just over a mile. He was well into the second of his planned four laps when he noticed another jogger about fifty yards in front of him, running in the same direction. Gradually, the distance between him and the other runner narrowed; as he got closer, Paul's competitive spirit kicked in. The runner in front was now his target, his quarry.

Paul put in a short kick of speed to reduce the gap, now less than twenty-five yards. Encouraged by the ease of his gains, Paul kicked again. This time, the distance between the two men didn't change. He upped his pace even more, but still the gap didn't close. Before he realised it, he was sprinting. The leg cadence of the runner in front did not seem to alter and yet, if anything, the 25 yards gap had grown.

Paul slowed, breathing heavily and trying desperately to maintain some kind of reasonable momentum. This guy was fit – too fit for Paul.

He dropped his pace even more, until he was moving at no more than a quick walk. The gap between himself and the other jogger narrowed...twenty yards...fifteen yards...ten yards. Bent over, with his hands on his knees and gasping for breath, Paul stopped. He lifted his head, knowing only too well what he would see.

"Oh, come on, Paul!" Simon said, "Here's you, fit and healthy and full of life, and I'm dead! You should be ashamed of yourself."

Paul tried to find the breath to utter some choice obscenities.

"Not as much fun as our last race, but a whole lot healthier, I suppose," Simon grinned.

"What do you want?" Paul managed, finally finding the strength to straighten his body. "You promised that you'd leave me alone. Just piss off and haunt somebody else, can't you?"

"If only it were that simple," Simon sighed. "There's a lot you'll have to learn about being dead, and that's what I can't understand. I've been thinking a lot about you. In just a few months, you've died twice, and yet here you are – alive and well. I know that you've died twice because of your two visits to The Chair. The living aren't allowed in there! So I'm beginning to wonder if you're holding out on me, Paul. I'm beginning to wonder if you know how to cheat death. Coming back from the dead once could be accepted as just being lucky. But *twice,* Paul? That's more than luck. What's the secret? I'd like to come back too, you see!"

Paul looked straight into the smiling eyes. "This is madness! I haven't died and you're not really here. I don't know why I'm being stupid enough to talk to you. It was all a dream – so this must be a dream. Do what you like, Simon. Even if I knew a way of cheating death, I wouldn't let you in on the secret. Go to hell! I'm done with you!"

"But I'm not done with you. A dream, am I? You think I'm just a dream? Dear me, Paul, you have more to learn than I thought. I think we need to see a lot more of each other – get to know each other better. Maybe then you'll realise that I'm much more than a dream. We'll talk again soon. You'll be desperate to talk to me again soon. You'll see!"

Before Paul had time to reply, Simon had turned and started jogging away. Paul watched as he rounded the curve of the path ahead, and disappeared from view.

Paul continued his run at his normal jogging pace. He looked, and watched, and listened, wondering if his demon would reappear...though he knew that he wouldn't. He tried to formulate a plan of action – but how could you plan against the unknown?

When Paul got home, Jo immediately asked him what was wrong.

"Just not feeling great," Paul replied. He hadn't realised that the effect of his meeting with Simon was so apparent in his mood.

"I thought that jogging was supposed to free the mind and stimulate the body?" Jo said, joking.

Paul didn't laugh. "Maybe I've picked up a bug or something," he said. "I'm not really hungry, Jo. I think I'll just get into a hot bath and have an early night. See if I can shake this off."

"That's fine. I haven't cooked yet. Go and have a soak and see how you feel."

Paul had the bath water as hot as he could bear. He lay back with a flannel over his eyes and tried to make some sense of what had happened.

He felt a sudden chill and sat up.

As the flannel fell from his face, he saw Simon, sitting just a few feet away on the closed toilet seat.

"Jesus!" he shouted.

"You alright?" Jo called up the stairs. "Did you want something?"

"No. I'm fine, love, just got the water from the tap a bit too hot."

"Just checking in," Simon said. "Don't worry – Jo can't hear me. Hope you enjoyed your run. We must do it again. I like racing."

Not knowing what to say or do, Paul lay back and put the flannel over his eyes again.

"See you soon, Paul."

The next time Paul looked, Simon had gone.

Paul went straight to bed and managed a troubled sleep.

When Jo came to tidy the bathroom, which she knew would be left in a dreadful mess, the white toilet seat was covered in a pale grey stain. As she watched in horror, the stain began to fade.

Jo forgot her tidying and went back downstairs. Were Paul's mood and the "stain" on the toilet seat connected? He'd been upset before taking his bath, but it was hard to believe that there wasn't something going on. What was Paul not telling her? Why was she not telling Paul? Could she talk to him about it? Should she talk to him? She didn't want to make things worse by dragging up the past if, from Paul's point of view, this had nothing to do with the past.

When morning came, Paul seemed to be fine. They breakfasted together and Jo went off to school. Neither of them mentioned the events of the previous evening. Both of them had a lot on their minds.

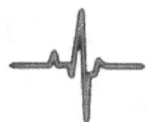

Chapter 35

Over the next few weeks, things became unbearable for Paul.

Wherever he went, Simon was there. The only blessing was that, since that one occasion in the bathroom, for some reason, Simon stayed out of the house. Paul would see him in the garden or standing in the front drive...sometimes he would see him sitting in the parked car, but never inside the home.

Whenever he went jogging, Simon would always be fifty yards in front of him. Sometimes his demon would allow the gap to shorten, but he would never let Paul catch up.

Paul would see him at the side of the road when he was out driving. He would see him at the supermarket and at the cinema, but Simon would always be far enough away to make it impossible for Paul to speak to him.

These constant intrusions into Paul's everyday life made him wary of going anywhere or doing anything. Jo was becoming frustrated with him. If she suggested going out for a meal or to see friends, Paul would find an excuse not to go. The house became his only safe haven.

The final straw came when Simon turned up at an audition Paul attended with Birmingham's prestigious theatre company. Simon sat behind the director and the producer of the new play and applauded wildly at all the wrong moments during Paul's performance. Needless to say, Paul was overlooked for the part.

Paul could see his whole life disintegrating. His relationship with Jo was becoming more and more fragile. She was spending more time with Sally, just to get away from his moods. He was increasingly loath to leave the safety of his own four walls. He stopped jogging. He stopped caring about anything. He was depressed. He even began thinking that death might not be a bad thing.

It was after another night alone in the house that Paul was finally forced to react.

Jo had been out with Sally. She returned home late and it was obvious from the moment she walked in that they were going to fight.

"I've had enough, Paul," she began, in a calm voice, "We can't go on like this. You have to tell me what's going on in your head. You've changed so much. You're not the man that I loved and married anymore. We're not even husband and wife – we just live in the same house. For God's sake, Paul – tell me! What's wrong with you?"

Confrontation was the last thing that Paul needed, but he could see that there was no walking away from this. "Sit down, Jo. Please, let's not fight. I know that I'm being impossible to live with. I don't want it to be that way, but I can't do anything about it. This is going to sound terribly corny, but I am the way that I am because I want to protect you."

"You're not protecting me. You're driving me away. This *is* all about your accident, I assume?"

"It's all so complicated," Paul said with his head in his hands. "Yes, it's all related to the accident, but not in any way that you'd imagine."

"Then just tell me. Let me in. Explain to me. Maybe I can help. Even if I can't, at least let me know what's ruining my life."

"Give me twenty-four hours, Jo – one day to sort this mess out. After that, I'll either tell you everything or telling you won't matter anymore."

"No, Paul! You're not going to walk away from this, not even for twenty-four hours. I'm at the end of my rope. You tell me now or I won't be here tomorrow."

Paul was silent for a moment. Without any further explanation, he said, "I'm going for a run."

"Were you listening to me?" she screamed. "Did you hear what I just said, Paul? I said I'm leaving. Does that not warrant more of a response than "I'm going for a run"? For Christ's sake! What planet are you on? Go for your bloody run! When you get back, I won't be here. But that doesn't matter, does it? You don't need me around to interfere in your own little world!"

"Jo..." Paul started, but she was already on her way upstairs.

Minutes later she was back, carrying a small case. "I'll be with Sally, if you're at all interested. I really don't want to hear from you until you're ready to tell me the truth, and I mean the whole truth. I suggest you don't leave it too long!"

Paul could not even look her in the eye.

The front door slammed, and she was gone.

For over an hour, Paul sat and did nothing. He didn't even think about the turn that his life had just taken. He was mentally drained. He closed his eyes and tried to sleep.

"Wow! That's buggered it!" a voice said.

Paul knew of the term "the red mist," but never in his life had he experienced the overwhelming anger that he felt when he saw the grinning face and heard the condescending tone from the armchair opposite him.

He flew at Simon. "Not in my house!" he screamed. "Don't you ever come in my house again!"

By the time he reached his target Simon was standing on the other side of the room.

"Calm down, Paul, you know that violence isn't in your nature. Sorry about Jo, honestly I am. I thought that you might be ready for that chat, but if you want me to leave, I'll go."

"You stay exactly where you are," Paul said, his voice trembling with rage. "We're going to sort this out, once and for all. Don't even think about moving!"

"That's what I like to hear, Paul. You see, I told you that you'd be wanting to talk to me again before long."

Paul sat down again and looked at Simon. How he detested that grinning face!

He tried to compose himself. He told himself that this was what he wanted: a showdown with his demon.

"Okay, Simon, or whatever your real name was, you're not a dream – you're a dead person, a ghost, a spirit. What are you? Let's get that bit straight to start with."

"Dead person will do fine," Simon grinned. "At least we've manage to get you to accept that part of the situation."

"So, dead person, I'll ask you again. What do want? Why are you here? What have I done to deserve this?"

"Let's take those questions in reverse order," Simon answered. "What have you done to deserve this? That one's easy. You killed me, remember? Why am I here? Well, right now I'm here because I thought you might want to talk, what with Jo leaving and everything. Last, but by no means least, what do I want? I told you that the last time we talked. What I want is my life back, and I do believe you can help me with that, Paul."

"Don't give me all that crap again – all that bullshit about me cheating death twice. I'm alive. I don't know how or why I'm alive. Ask the doctors who treated me. There's no secret formula for coming back from the dead. That's just crazy. I can't help you. Believe me, right now I'd do anything to get you out of my life for good, but I can't help you, Simon. You're dead. Live with it!"

"That's good," Simon laughed. "Very droll. 'Live with it!' I like that. The problem is, I'd like to believe you but I can't. I really don't like being dead, Paul. It's a bore. If I hadn't got you to play with, I don't know what I'd do with myself. You must be able to understand that if there's the slightest chance you could help get my life back, then I've got to pursue that chance."

"This is going nowhere," Paul sighed. "How can I ever convince you that there's nothing I can do for you?"

"I've actually thought long and hard about that, and do you know what? I can only think of one way that we're going to be able to sort this out."

"Tell me," Paul begged. "Tell me what it is. Anything – I'll do anything you ask. Just get out of my life!"

"It's a pretty drastic remedy. I'm not sure that you'll be very keen to go for it, but it really is the only way."

"Christ!" Paul shouted, his anger rising again. "*What* is the only remedy? What have I got to do to get rid of you?"

"You have to die again, Paul! Surely three strikes and you're out! If you beat it again, you'll find out what the secret is. You'll be looking for it this time. One more death scene, Paul. I've seen you acting; you're good. One more death scene. If you do end up dead, too bad – if you live, then you might be able to help me live too. I know I'm being selfish, but it's the only way. So what do you think? If you live, you get Jo back. Are you ready to die again for Jo?"

"You are insane! Just get out of my house. I'll find a way to deal with you. I'll have you exorcised or something. Just go. Talk's over!"

"I knew you'd need time to think about it, so I'll leave you in peace for a few days. But when I come back, I'll need an answer. By the way, exorcism is just for the movies, Paul. It doesn't really work. I'm afraid you're stuck with me. Think about it – death or glory! The drama should appeal to you. I'll be back in seven days; that should give you plenty of time for thought."

Simon left the room through the door, just as any normal human being would have done. There was no disappearing into thin air. He just walked out, leaving Paul with his thoughts.

The Chair

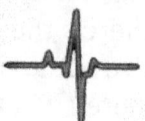

Chapter 36

When Paul awoke the next morning, he was still sitting in the living room armchair.

It took him a few moments to remember all that had happened the night before. For a brief instant, he thought it had all been a bad dream and that soon Jo would be coming downstairs to start making breakfast.

He checked his watch: 9.30am. Jo would already be in school – she'd have woken him if she had been in the house. This was no dream.

What about Simon? Was that part a dream? One week to decide if he wanted to die – he must have dreamt that part.

He climbed the stairs to the bathroom. As soon as he opened the door, he saw it: 7 DAYS was written in condensation on the mirror. He leaned against the washbasin and stared at the writing. In anger, he wiped his palm across the writing to erase it from view. Nothing happened. The mirror still read "7 DAYS." He turned his back on the message and stared at the bathroom door. Nature reminded him why he had come to the bathroom. He turned and lifted the toilet seat. As relief came, he realised that the message had gone.

Paul made coffee – strong black coffee. He sat at the kitchen table, his mind in complete turmoil. From the depths of his soul, a low, mournful groan reached his throat. He was beaten. It had to be over.

He remembered Jo's words: "I'm at the end of my rope." Suddenly, his mind was clear.

Out in the garage, Paul lifted the coil of blue nylon rope from the hook on the wall. The rope that had been used as a prop in an amateur dramatic society production, the rope that had towed the Audi out of a snow drift two years ago, the rope he had found fallen from a lorry in the middle of the road, the rope he had stopped and picked up thinking that it may come in handy one day. He could never have imagined the use to which it was about to be put.

He threw the blue coil into the back of the car and went back into the kitchen.

His coffee was still warm enough to drink. He made toast, and even managed a smile. Paul was amazed at how calm he was feeling. There wasn't a single doubt in his mind. This was the right thing to do, but he must do it properly. He must do it in a way that would bring as little distress as possible to the ones he loved, especially to Jo!

He found a notepad and pen and pondered for a moment before he started writing. Somehow, even the words he used seem to come to mind without any difficulty, almost as if it was preordained that this should be his fate.

Dear Jo,
I'm so sorry, but this was the only way for me.
My mind is tormented. I can never be the man you knew again.
I don't know yet where they will find me. At least I will be at peace.
Try not to hate me, Jo. I love you so much!
Paul. X

He folded the note and left it tucked under the empty coffee mug on the kitchen table.

As he passed the hall mirror, he stopped to take one last look at himself. The drawn, unshaven face that looked back at him made him close his eyes sharply. The image just confirmed that what he was about to do was totally necessary.

He was reaching for the handle of the front door when the doorbell rang. The chime seemed to jolt him awake. He stepped back from the door, not wanting to answer, not wanting any interruption to his plans. He waited. After a few seconds the bell chimed again. He realised that his car was parked in the drive. Whoever it was would know that he was in. Reluctantly, he opened the door.

"Surprise!" Robin Thomas shouted, with arms outstretched and a huge grin on his face. "I was in Birmingham last night, so I thought I'd look you up this morning and see how you're getting on. Wouldn't be much of an agent if I didn't keep an eye on my assets. Christ, Paul. You look bloody awful. Come on, buddy – let me in. Get the kettle on!"

"Robin...good to see you, Come in, man. You should have let me know you were in the area."

"Wouldn't have been a surprise then, would it?" Robin joked. "Seriously, Paul, you don't look great. Are you alright?"

"I'm fine. Just a bad night, I guess. How long are you around for?" Without thinking, Paul led the way into the kitchen. Remembering the note he had left on the table, he made an obvious dive to grab it before Robin sat down. He screwed the note up and threw it into the waste bin.

"Got to get back to London by this evening, unfortunately, but I've got a few hours. The flight out of Birmingham is around five o'clock. How's Jo?"

"Jo's fine. She's in school. Won't be back until teatime. You want tea or coffee?"

"Coffee's fine. So tell me, what's been going on?"

Paul needed time to think. He filled the kettle. "Must just pop to the loo," he said. "Won't be a minute. Make yourself at home."

By the time Paul returned, Robin had the note he had thrown away in his hands. "What the hell is this crap!" he shouted at Paul, waving the note in the air.

"Bastard!" Paul yelled. "You had no right to read that. Who the hell do you think you are? Get out!"

"I'll tell you who the hell I am. I'm your friend. I'm Jo's friend too. Remember me? Robin Thomas? We go way back, Paul. Now I'll ask you again. What the hell is this crap?"

He slammed the piece of paper down on the kitchen table.

"Just go, Robin. Please, just go and forget that you ever came here today."

"I'm going nowhere, man – and you're going nowhere too until you've explained this bullshit to me!" He picked up the note again and read, "'My mind is tormented. At least I will be at peace.' Jesus Christ, Paul! What are you thinking of?"

Paul slumped into a chair and held his head in his hands. "Why did you have to come, Robin? Today of all days. Why did you have to come?"

Seeing the state that his friend was in, Robin softened his voice. "Bloody good job I did come, by the looks of things. Talk to me Paul. For God's sake, talk to me!"

Over the next two hours, Paul confided in his friend. Robin demanded every detail and Paul kept nothing back. By the time he had reached the moment of Jo leaving and his last meeting with Simon, he was exhausted.

Robin stood up and moved round the table to where Paul was sitting. He silently hugged his troubled friend. After a few moments, he returned to his seat at the other side of the table. He reached across and took Paul's hand.

"You know what I'm going to say, Paul. You need help. Good professional help. It's easy for me to say that you shouldn't have let things go this far without telling someone, but that doesn't help now. What you were planning is just madness. That's over now. Now that you've shared your torment with me, that plan is over. We have to find a different way."

"There is no other way, Robin. Do you think that I want to die? Do you think that I want to do this to Jo, to my parents? Shrinks aren't going to help me. Simon will still be here – haunting me. I can't live with that any longer."

"We have a problem then. You don't think for one minute that I'm about to let my best mate go out and top himself, do you? We need time to think about this and to talk some more. I'm going to stay with you. Everything else can go to hell as far as I'm concerned. From what you've told me, we have seven days before Simon reappears. Let's at least give ourselves that time to try to find another way. Promise me you won't do anything for these seven days – for old time's sake, Paul, at least give me that promise."

Paul thought for a moment. "You have my word," he finally said, "but only on this condition. You talk to no one about what I've told you. You don't contact any shrinks. You don't talk to Jo or my parents. No one! *We* have to find an answer, Robin, just you and me. And if we can't, you have to let me handle things my own way. Do we have a deal?"

"We have a deal that I will talk to no one, but there's no way that I can promise you that I'll just walk away in seven days time if we haven't come up with something. You can't demand that of me, Paul."

"Then let's hope that we can find another way. In seven days time, Simon will be back. Don't think that he isn't aware that you are here right now. He's always going to be one step ahead of me. I don't know how we can deal with that, but I'll give you the seven days, for old time's sake."

Robin called British Airways and cancelled his evening flight. He managed to talk Paul into taking a nap. When he was sure that his friend was asleep, he sat on the couch and went over every detail of what Paul had told him.

Now Robin had his own demons to deal with. To what extent could he keep a promise to a friend who was so obviously mentally disturbed? If he broke the promise, he might save a life but lose the friend. Was that life worth saving or would he be condemning someone he loved to a lifetime of misery and torment? If he kept his promise, was it right or even helpful to humour this fantasy – to pretend that he believed that this fantasy was real and could be dealt with? These questions consumed his thoughts.

"What in God's name am I going to do?"

He closed his eyes and slept too.

Chapter 37

Robin was awakened by the sound of Paul moving around. He was delighted to find his friend in much higher spirits than before. He had shaved and changed and looked much more like his old self.

Paul confirmed that he felt better for having confided in Robin. He still doubted that anything could be done about Simon, but, whatever the outcome, somebody else now understood what he was going through.

Robin decided on a conservative approach. He would humour his friend, to some extent. He would discuss ways that they might deal with Paul's demon, but at the same time he would try to convince Paul that professional counselling would be helpful. He hoped that seven days would be long enough for him to talk Paul out of his suicidal intentions.

The extreme tension that had prevailed when Paul was telling his story had gone. Robin and Paul were able to chat in a calm and normal way about a situation that was anything but calm or normal. It was impossible to talk about anything else.

Robin confessed to Paul that he was having misgivings about the promise that he had made to say nothing to anyone. He wanted to see how Paul would react. "You've made me feel like a bloody priest! I'm bound to secrecy by the terms of the confessional."

"I must trust you to keep your word, just as you must trust me to keep mine."

"Maybe we both need counselling," Robin tried. "You to sort your head out, and me to sort out the morality of keeping a promise that may have devastating effects."

"Perhaps we should just be each other's counsel, at least for the next seven days."

"Can't argue with that," Robin said grudgingly.

The day was gone in a flash. Darkness had fallen.

"What do we do about grub?" Robin asked, "I'm starving. Let's go out and find a meal. You can show me the delights of Wolverhampton's night life."

"I'm not sure that Wolverhampton has a nightlife," Paul laughed, "but I could certainly eat something too."

"Do one thing for me Paul, before we go out. Give Jo a call and tell her you're okay. Tell her I'm with you. You don't have to go into detail. Just tell her that we're sorting things out. It can't do any harm. I'm sure that she's climbing the walls worrying about you. Put her mind at rest. Please!"

"She won't talk to me, Robin. You don't know her like I do. You're right that she'll be in a state, worrying. But she's so stubborn – I know she won't talk to me."

"Then let me call her. You can listen to everything that I say. I'm not going to shop you. I hate to think of her wondering if you're okay. Let me try to put her mind at rest."

Paul reluctantly agreed and Robin picked up the phone. He kept his word and made the call as sterile as possible. Paul could tell that Jo was asking him all sorts of questions, but his friend managed to avoid any revealing answers. Both Robin and Paul were relieved when the call ended.

"Right. What's on the menu then? How about a nice hot curry?"

"Sounds good to me," Paul said, and the two went out to eat.

Paul realised that this was the first time he had been out of the house for many days. God knows why, but he trusted Simon not to make an appearance and he spent a semi-relaxed evening with his old friend.

Over their meal the two agreed that tomorrow they would get their heads together and try to come to terms with Paul's problems. Both knew that simply doing that was only going to lead to further problems, but for Paul, it was good to have found the support of his friend, and for Robin, the process of saving *his* good friend had to begin somewhere.

An excellent meal and few too many beers encouraged a good night's sleep for both. There would be much to do the following day.

Chapter 38

By the time Paul came downstairs the next morning, Robin was already onto his third mug of coffee.

"Bloody hell!" Robin said. "Are these the hours that actors normally keep? It's gone eleven o'clock – I must be in the wrong business. I've usually done a day's work by now, looking after layabouts like you!"

"Good morning to you, too!" Paul yawned. "What's up, mate? Couldn't you sleep? I remember the days at drama school when I had to drag you from your pit at teatime to get ready for the next party!"

"Touché!" Robin laughed. "Yes, those were the days. The most important things in life were the three "S's": Sleep, Sex, and Shakespeare, though not necessarily in that order. Listen, mate. Whilst you've been festering in *your* pit, I've been thinking; I've come up with an idea. The kettle's just boiled. Make us both a coffee and I'll reveal all."

"You've got coffee," Paul said, pointing at the mug in front of Robin.

"That one's dead – re-fill needed. Hurry up. I want to hear what you think of my revelation."

Paul placed a fresh mug of coffee in front of his friend and took the chair opposite. "Okay, Mr Freud! Let's hear your fiendish plan to rid me of my demons. But I'm telling you now, if it involves a shrink, I'll pour that coffee over your head!"

Robin raised both his palms, "No shrink," he promised, "just you and your demon."

"Shoot!" Paul said.

This is going to be difficult to explain. If it begins to sound crazy, stop me and I'll try to find a way to make it clearer."

"Just get on with it, will you?"

"Before I do 'get on with it,' I'm going to be totally honest with you, Paul, because I need to feel that, whatever happens, I tried to do the right things. I think that this whole Simon thing is a load of bollocks!"

"Well, thanks for the support," Paul said, disappointed.

"Let me finish, Paul. Put yourself in my place and you'd come to the same conclusion. However, I also am totally convinced that even though *I* think that Simon is a load of bollocks, for you, Simon is very real and has to be dealt with."

"Point taken," Paul agreed. "Sorry, mate. I didn't mean to sound ungrateful."

"Apology accepted," Robin said. "So, I've been going over everything that you've told me and I've come up with two points in your story that warrant particular consideration.

"I guess what we're trying to do is separate fantasy from reality. In a dream, anything is possible. You know what I mean. You might have a pink rabbit talking to a purple elephant and it would seem perfectly normal if you were dreaming."

"You must have some wacky weird dreams," Paul laughed. "I reckon it's you that needs a shrink!"

"I'll ignore that for the moment. Please just bear with me. I told you that this would be difficult. Okay, so in a dream the ridiculous appears to be sensible and the impossible appears possible, but as soon as you wake up and apply logic to your dream, you realise that it had to be just a dream no matter how real it felt at the time. Are you with me so far?"

"Yes, I'm still here!"

"Let's go back to the pink rabbit and the purple elephant. I am 100% certain that that's a dream unless someone can show me a pink rabbit and a purple elephant having a conversation. Would you agree with that?"

"All the way," Paul said. "Do go on."

"I said that there were two parts of your story that deserved particular scrutiny. The first part is the fact that Simon is so clever. He's always 'one step ahead,' as you said. He already 'knows that I'm with you.' This guy knows everything. We can't pull the wool over his eyes. Right?"

"Correct."

"The other part of your story to look at is the accident that you had when Simon was with you in the car – the second time you 'died.' Remember the pink rabbit again – show me a pink talking rabbit and I'll agree that it may not have been a dream. Okay. Show me a crashed car and a police accident report and maybe a few eyewitnesses and I'll believe that there was a fatal accident on the M6 that night – an accident in which you died. There was no wreck, Paul. There was no police involvement, no eyewitnesses. You'd have told me if there were. You have to agree that the pink rabbit hasn't been produced. You have to agree that accident was only in your head - a dream!

"I'm guessing that you had reached that assumption yourself, but that maybe, with everything else that's going on in your head, you hadn't realised the significance of your assumption."

"Yes," Paul said, "I had sort of realised that the accident with Simon never really happened, but where does that leave us? I'm not getting the full point."

"Back to our genius, Simon – this guy who knows everything and is convinced that you have died and come back to life twice. We can't dispute that you may have 'died' temporarily in the first accident; even the doctors can't tell us that for sure. What we do know for certain is that your death in the second accident was all part of a dream – a dream that clever Simon believes to be true. Simon has to be your 'pink rabbit,' Paul. It's very convenient, don't you think, that no one else can see or hear him and that he can't haunt anyone who didn't know him."

"I hear what you're getting at, Robin, but the fact that Simon was in that dream doesn't mean he isn't real. I could have seen you in that dream. That wouldn't mean that you don't exist."

"Quite right," Robin agreed, "but if I had been in that dream, would you expect me, in reality, to believe what happened in the dream? How would I even know what happened? It was your dream – not mine! You're trying to tell me that the Simon whom you believe to be real led you into a dream that was unreal and yet he believes what happened in that dream to be true. Surely you can see that just doesn't add up - even for a ghost!"

"So what you're saying is that if Simon is part of reality, he wouldn't believe in or wouldn't even be aware that he had figured in my dream of the second accident."

"Exactly. And the fact that your Simon *does* believe that you died in that accident means that he has to be a part of an ongoing fantasy that's raging in your head."

"That all sounds absolutely logical, Robin, until Simon is standing in front of me in seven days' time. He will be here, you know!"

"He's a pink rabbit Paul, but to you he's a very real pink rabbit, and yes, he probably will be here, but we have the advantage on him now."

"What do you mean by 'advantage'? I don't understand."

"If he's not real, Paul, he can't physically hurt you. He can't actually kill you. He might take you through another dream where you die. So what? You'll wake up and you'll be very much alive and kicking and, who knows, going through that 'final death scene' as you say he put it so dramatically may finally rid you of his presence for good."

"So in a week's time I say, 'Okay, Simon, I'm ready to die again if that will get you out of my life forever'? Is that what you're suggesting?"

"Well, it beats the hell out of suicide, Paul. Simon can't hurt you, and if going through this charade can rid your mind of this pink rabbit, it has to be worth a shot."

"Then that's what I'll do, my friend," Paul said. "But if I die, I'll come back and haunt you – you can be sure of that!"

The two remained silent for several minutes, each with his thoughts on what might happen. Paul was the first to speak. "There's one bit of all this that doesn't add up. If Simon's my pink rabbit, how does he know that I died for a short time in the first accident? That accident certainly was a part of reality."

Robin turned to Paul with a strange look on his face. "But we have no proof that you did die in that crash. In any case, Simon knows exactly what *you* want him to know to fuel your fantasy."

"All the same, something is bothering you, isn't it, Robin? I can see it in your face. No wonder you took up management instead of acting. You're an open book. What about The Chair, Robin, Is it The Chair that's bothering you?"

"More coffee I think," Robin said, avoiding the question. "More coffee and then out for a spot of lunch."

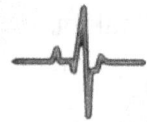

Chapter 39

It was at lunch that day when strange things began to happen. Many of these things could have been easily explained away in different circumstances.

Paul and Robin were enjoying their pub meals, when a very large spider fell into Robin's pint of lager. The creature had such long legs that it was able to extricate itself from the layer of white froth onto which it had fallen and climb out of the glass and onto the table. The two friends joked as the spider made its escape on what, both of them were sure, were very wobbly legs.

When Robin replaced his contaminated pint, Paul placed a beer mat over the top of his new glass. "Can't be too careful!" he said, giving Robin a knowing look.

Robin dismissed the incident but left the beer mat on top of his glass.

A few minutes later, an equally large spider fell onto the beer mat and scuttled quickly away.

The two men looked at each other but said nothing.

Robin experienced other incidents. Things were moved. His can of shaving cream turned up on his pillow, his shoes ended up on opposite sides of his room. Robin wondered if Paul was playing pranks on him but was afraid to challenge his friend in case the answer was no. If he told Paul what had happened, it would inevitably strengthen his friend's case for Simon being a part of reality.

Then there was the incident with his toothbrush: it simply disintegrated, leaving him with a mouth full of bristles. He failed to see how Paul could have been behind that.

Each time something occurred, Robin became less certain that the plan he and Paul had agreed on was safe to carry out. He was becoming increasingly convinced that Simon was not just a figment of Paul's imagination. He wrestled with the problem, but always came up with the same answer. He told himself that he was becoming paranoid and that his original assessment of the situation had to be correct. In any case, if he tried to stop Paul from agreeing to Simon's demand that he should die again, Robin had no Plan B to fall back on.

For the next four days, Paul and Robin lived in each other's pockets, neither wanting to give the other the chance to go back on their promises. Robin could hardly believe how calm and relaxed Paul seemed to be. Paul could not help but notice that, as each day went by, Robin became more agitated.

With just two of the seven days left, things came to a head.

Robin had suggested going to the local shopping centre to buy some clothes. He was tired of borrowing sweaters and shirts from Paul. The overnight bag he had brought with him contained only one change. How could he have known that he would be staying for a week?

Paul was happy to accompany his friend. Robin said he also needed to find a birthday card for a colleague and he would get the address from his briefcase upstairs before they set off.

When Robin entered his bedroom, the briefcase, which had been left on a bedside chair, was lying open on the floor, its contents spread around the room. The case had been locked – he was absolutely certain. Even if it had fallen from the chair, it would not have sprung open; and, even if it had sprung open, his papers could never have been so widely spread about. He stared at the mess. He shouted to Paul to come up.

Paul looked at the open briefcase and at the papers that were strewn around. "I know that you have to ask the question," he said, turning to face Robin, "but the answer is no! I had nothing to do with this. I'm not going to say 'I told you so,' but I did tell you."

"We need to talk!" Robin said with a very worried look on his face, "This changes everything."

"Wrong!" Paul replied. "This changes nothing, Robin. I've known all along that Simon is real. Now you've found out too – but it changes nothing."

"Don't be ridiculous! If there really is a Simon who is after your life, you need protection. We need to call in some help, Paul."

"Oh yes! And, 'who ya gonna call - Ghostbusters?' Think about it. You'll end up getting us both certified. Let's just stick to what we agreed. I'm going to fire some logic at you now, Robin. Simon isn't going to want to harm me. I'm too valuable to him. I'm his only way back."

"That doesn't work, and you know it! Simon will be quite happy to risk your life, or death, simply because there's no other way back for him. He'll kill you, Paul, just to see what happens next."

"Possibly, but five days ago, I was about to do that for him anyway. We don't have another option, buddy. I knew that all along. I'm still holding you to your promise not to involve anyone else. Break your word and I'll break mine too – and you know what that means."

"For God's sake, Paul, I can't just stand by and watch you get killed!"

"Then go back to London, Robin. I'll understand. You won't be deserting me."

"There has to be another way. Let's just both calm down and think."

At that moment, two mobile phones rang. Both men reached in their pockets and took out their phones. Both phones felt like blocks of ice. Both screens were blank. Both looked as if they had been torched from inside. Both mobiles were useless.

Paul went downstairs to check the house phone. He lifted the receiver. The phone was dead. Robin had followed him into the room. "We're being isolated," Paul said.

"We're not prisoners!" Robin snapped. "He can't stop us making outside contact. This is crazy!"

"Sit down Robin. Sit down and listen to me. The only thing that has changed is that you are now willing to believe that Simon is not just part of a dream. You can't see him, but you can see what he can do. This is all a game for him. He's bored. He told me so. It's a game that he can't lose because he really is always one step ahead. We have no idea what his limitations are so we have no real way of getting the better of him. That leaves us with two choices – to do what he asks or for me to spend a life being constantly watched and taunted by a dead person. I'm not prepared to lead that life."

"There has to be something we can do."

"We do exactly as we planned," Paul said, "because Simon will not let us do anything else. I still believe that we do have one ace up our sleeve."

"Then, for God's sake, tell me what it is!"

"Our ace is this. Simon has proved that he can haunt me. He can be everywhere I go. Watch everything I do. He can wreck my whole life. He can haunt you too, but I'm hoping that is only the case when you are with me – otherwise, you are in as much danger as I am. I said before that we don't know his limitations, but that isn't strictly true. One thing we can be fairly sure of is that he can't kill me. If he could, why would he be asking me to agree to die? Why wouldn't he just get rid of me without my consent? That would serve his purpose just as well. No! I know that Simon can destroy me mentally, but I'm confident that he can't physically harm me. He has to make me do that to myself. I have no idea how we should play our ace. All I can think of is that we go along with Simon's wishes and hope that, when the time comes, we recognise our opportunity."

"It's too risky, Paul. This is your life you're gambling with."

"I don't have a life as long as Simon is around. I've already accepted that fact. I either die with him or I live without him – that's the offer he's made. I have no choice, Robin. We have no choice. My big regret is that I have got you involved in all of this. We have two days left. Let's stop thinking about three days from now. You're a good friend, Robin. Please, just help me do what has to be done."

"It's your call. I hate it - but it *is* your call. If I lose you, I'll never forgive myself. But if I manage to stop you, I will be condemning you to lifelong misery – and I can't do that. We'll meet your demon together, and if I have to watch my best friend die, I'll do that for you too."

Robin stood up and threw his arms around his friend. There were no more words to be said.

As they hugged, two mobile phones rang. Both screens were displaying "caller's name withheld." Both phones felt normal to the touch. Both men rejected the calls. The house phone rang. There was no one there.

"Bet your briefcase has been tidied up too!" Paul said, and when the two of them went to check, it was back on the bedside chair, lid open, but all contents neatly restored.

"I wonder why he left the lid open?" Robin said.

"It's a game," Paul answered. "You have to remember, it's just a game."

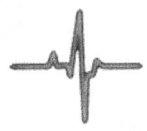

Chapter 40

The Japanese have a saying: "Truth is found between sleep and waking." There is a brief moment between the two, when the mind arouses from sleep to when it realises full consciousness. At that moment, the mind is defenceless and only truth can be revealed.

In reverse, sleep depravation is used with great success as a method of interrogation. Torture it may be, but when the mind is slipping into sub-consciousness, it finds subterfuge impossible.

As he awoke on the morning of the seventh day, everything in Robin's mind told him to stop this madness. Chain Paul to a chair, drug him, lock him up, but do not let him be driven to his death by the spectre of a dead man.

But now he was fully awake and he knew that the day would take its course, whatever that course might be.

The Spanish have a phrase: "*Que sera sera*." Robin prayed that the Spanish had got it right and that the Japanese were mistaken.

He could hear Paul moving about downstairs. Robin tried to imagine how Paul would be feeling. Could he really be that confident that the "ace up his sleeve" would prove to be the beating of his demon?

He showered and dressed. Just to remind him that he was helpless to interfere, Robin found that, when he came to put his shoes on, the laces had been tied together. He was just a pawn in Simon's game. "I can tie you up in knots," Simon was saying to him. Robin couldn't argue with that.

Downstairs, Paul had made coffee. He took out a second mug and filled it for Robin.

"So when do you expect Simon to appear?" Robin asked, as casually as he could.

"He's already been," Paul replied, equally casually. "He was here when I woke about an hour ago. Said it would be easier for me to talk freely without you being around."

"Need I ask what you told him?" Robin said, slightly miffed that he had missed the visit.

"I told him exactly what we decided – not that he didn't already know. You really must stop worrying, Robin. This is going to happen. This scene is going to be played out - one way or another."

"How can you be so calm? You don't even seem to be considering that this day may be your last. I'm in pieces and you're acting as if this really is just a game."

"I must be a better actor than I thought." Paul replied, with half a smile. "Of course I have my misgivings about this whole charade but – quite simply – I have nowhere else to go. Today is a win/win day for me, Robin. Today I lose my demon – that's definite."

"You call losing your life winning?"

"I've already lost my life. Simon has already taken it away from me. Today I get the chance to take it back, and that's what I call winning."

"You know what? Ninety-nine percent of the time I'd say that, mentally, you were perfectly normal. This is the other one percent. When I hear you talk this way, I'm convinced that you're totally off your head."

Robin walked out of the kitchen, unable to take any more. Paul let him go, aware of how difficult this must be for his friend. They had all day to talk. Simon's drama would not take to the stage until late into the night. That had already been decided.

The Chair

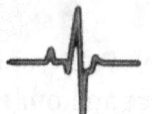

Chapter 41

All of Robin's prayers were answered when, at just after 11am, the front doorbell chimed and Paul let his father into the house.

It was obvious Mitch was not in the mood for messing around.

"What the hell is going on here, Paul? Your Mum and I have Jo on the phone telling us that she's moved out. You don't bother to call us, and when we try to ring you, the house phone's dead and you're not answering your mobile. I suggest that you start talking to me – and start talking right now!"

"I'll leave you two for a while," Robin said quietly, standing to leave.

"You'll sit right where you are!" Mitch shouted. "No one's going anywhere until I find out what's going on."

"Cool down, Dad, Robin's a guest in my house. Please don't speak to him like that."

"I'll cool down when I start getting some answers. So which one of you is going to start? Come on! I'm waiting!"

Robin looked at Paul. "If you don't tell him, I will. I don't want to break a promise to you, Paul, but this has gone far enough. Please. It's better coming from you."

Paul turned to his father. "How long have you got, Dad? This could take a while."

"I've got all night and then some," was the reply, "Will you please start talking!"

—⁄ᴧ⁄—

Paul began to explain. Mitch already knew much of the story from when Paul had come round from his coma. It wasn't long before Mitch butted in.

"Look, son, I thought we'd dealt with all this crap about two car accidents and ghosts and mysterious pubs for the dead. You need help, Paul. Come on, let's go and see if we can talk to Grayson."

"Hold on, Dad. I thought I'd dealt with it all too, but it's not as simple as that. Wait 'til you hear the rest of the story before you consign me to the madhouse. Robin thought I was bananas when he first came but I don't think he's of the same opinion now."

Both men looked at Robin who just held his hands up. "Just carry on, Paul. Mitch, I think you should listen."

When Paul had told his father everything, Mitch stood up.

He pointed first at his son. "You are ill!" Pointing at Robin, he said, "And you should have more sense than to be taken in by all this bullshit. I'm going to get help for you, son. Coat on; we're going to the hospital."

"No can do," Paul said. "Sorry, Dad, I know you mean well, but even you are out of your depth here."

"Fine!" Mitch sighed. "Then the hospital will have to come to you. You're going to sit right there until help arrives."

Mitch felt for his mobile. When he took it from his pocket, it was icy cold. The screen was blank and looked charred. "Bloody thing!" Mitch growled, throwing the phone on the table. Robin and Paul could immediately see what had happened.

Mitch was already at the house phone. "Why's this thing dead, Paul?"

"It was working fine earlier," Paul offered.

"Give me your mobile!" Mitch demanded.

Both Paul and Robin offered their mobiles to Mitch. Both phones were back to the state they had been in earlier – both useless.

"Is this some kind of stupid joke? Alright, I'll go to the hospital and bring help. You don't let him out of your sight!" he raged, pointing at Robin. "You make sure he's here, and in one piece when I get back or God help you!"

Robin said nothing.

"He won't let you do it, Dad. He'll find a way to stop you."

"Stop *me*?" Mitch laughed. "Your fantasy ghost is going to stop *me*! I don't think so."

Mitch made his way into the hall to the front door. It was only a couple of seconds before he yelled, "Unlock this bloody door, Paul. I've had enough of this pissing about!"

"It isn't locked, Dad. The key's in the door. Just turn the key if you think it's locked."

Mitch went straight to the back door. It too would not open.

Flustered, yet still refusing to believe, Mitch came back into the living room and picked up a dining chair and threatened to smash a window.

Paul grabbed his arm. "Put it down, Dad. It's time to take stock."

Mitch was shaking with rage. Paul helped him to an armchair and lowered him in.

"Maybe I'd better tell you my story," Robin said. "I haven't even told Paul all of this."

Robin began to recount all the strange things that had been happening to him over the last few days. "I'm not crazy, Mr Ford. I haven't suffered any head trauma. This is real. Much as I hate to say it, this is all very real!"

At that moment, three mobile phones and the house phone all began ringing.

"See what I mean?" Robin said, "Scary, isn't it?"

It still took a while before Mitch was willing to accept the possibility that Simon was real, but arguing against all that had happened was futile.

"I'm staying," he finally said. "I'll call your mum and tell her I'll be back tomorrow. I'll say nothing about what's gone on here."

"Yes, do that," Paul said. "We don't want her being so worried that she comes over too."

When the call had been made, Mitch looked at his son. "Sorry to have sounded off like I did. Sorry to you too, Robin. How long have we got before..."

"Not 'til late tonight." Paul answered. "It's up to me, really. When I'm ready, I just jump in the car and drive. Simon will join me and take over."

"Not another bloody car crash," Mitch said disbelievingly. "Has this idiot got no imagination?"

"Oh no!" Paul said. "No car crash this time, more 'a leap of faith.' Those were his words, not mine. That's all I know, so please don't ask. If you two insist on being there, I suggest you both follow in Dad's car."

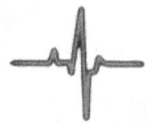

The mood for the rest of the afternoon was understandably sombre. They all picked at food from the fridge. They tried to talk about anything they could think of that didn't involve the next few hours. As darkness fell, all three just wanted this to be over and done with. Inside, all three were terrified.

Chapter 42

At 10.30pm, Paul stood up. All eyes followed him.

"I guess this is it!" he said. "Time to get this sorted. Wish me luck!"

Robin was first to stand and hug his friend. He could think of nothing to say, just a hug and a pat on the back. He stood aside to let Mitch get near to his son.

"We could still just drive to the hospital?" he said, imploring his boy to change his mind.

"Come on, Dad. We've been through all this. Even you must know that the answer doesn't lie at the hospital. Why don't you stay here 'til I come home? This must be even worse for you than it is for me."

"I'm sticking as close to you as I can," Mitch said. "I'll be there, with Robin, in case there's anything we can do."

"Thanks, Dad, but promise me – both of you – no interference! This has to be played out. This is my chance to get my life back. You can't do anything to take that chance away from me. I have no idea what's going to happen, but you two just stay in the car. I'll come to you when it's over."

Neither Mitch nor Robin replied. Paul took their silence as their word that they would not try to intervene.

As Paul got into his car, Mitch asked, "How will we know when Simon--?"

Paul stopped him. "Don't ask, Dad. I don't know the answer. Just follow, if you must, and watch – nothing more. I'll tell you when it's all over."

"Good luck, son! I love you!"

Mitch closed the door on Paul's car and walked to his own, which was parked in the street outside Paul's house. Robin and Mitch climbed into the Jaguar and followed Paul's Ford in silence.

The Ford headed towards town. Tailing it was easy. There was little other traffic at this time of night. They headed

189

along the Newhampton Road and then turned right towards West Park, Paul's favourite spot for jogging. They circuited the park three times, Mitch's Jaguar always staying at a reasonable distance behind the Ford.

"What's he doing?" Robin asked. "Maybe Simon hasn't turned up! Do you think we should flash him and get him to stop?"

"Best just follow," Mitch answered. "We don't know what's going on in that car."

On the fifth lap of West Park, things changed. Both left and right indicators on the Ford suddenly started flashing simultaneously. Mitch tried to edge closer to see if they could make out if anything was happening inside the car. The space between the cars remained constant. Mitch accelerated even more. The gap didn't alter.

"I guess this is it!" Mitch said, backing off his speed. "I don't think Paul's alone in that car anymore. I can't believe this is really happening. What do we do?"

"We trust in your son. We do what he asked of us. We let him try to get his life back. If necessary – we have to let him go. It's the way he wants it to be. We have to give him that much."

Another lap of West Park was completed before the Ford indicated to turn left, back towards Newhampton Road. Mitch followed as Paul made his way to the town centre. The Ford indicated left and turned into the shopping centre's multi-storey car park.

"Oh, my God!" Mitch gasped, as he tailed the Ford into the narrow entrance. "I've got a really bad feeling about this. 'A leap of faith.' Wasn't that what Paul said Simon had told him? This is pure, bloody madness, Robin. We have to stop this!"

―⌁―

The Chair

Simon had joined Paul during his third lap of West Park. He was smiling, as always, and obviously excited about the prospect of what was about to happen.

"Excellent choice of meeting place," he commented, as he settled into the passenger seat next to Paul. "Haven't seen you out jogging lately – you should take better care of your health!"

"Can we cut the small talk and get on with this?" Paul said, keeping his eyes firmly on the road ahead. "Where do you want me to go?"

"Oh come on Paul, don't be a party pooper. Where's your sense of fun, of anticipation? Surely you're excited about tonight too. There's no rush. Just drive a little whilst we chat."

"Fine! Chat away!" was Paul's response.

"You really are in a bad mood, aren't you? What's the matter? If this goes well you'll never see me again. Think how good that will feel!"

"Maybe I am mad. Here I am, driving round in circles, talking to a dead person about killing myself. How wacky is that? What's even funnier is that I trust the word of a ghost to stay out of my life! A shrink would have a field day with me!"

"Ah! Glad to hear you haven't lost you sense of humour! You really mustn't worry about me keeping my word. A deal's a deal, even for a dead person."

"Delighted to hear it!" Paul said sarcastically. "So where are we going?"

"Once more around the park and then we'll head off. Hang on, just going to flash your indicators to let Dad and Robin know that I've arrived. Nice of them to come with you."

"Just leave them out of this. This is between you and me. They won't interfere. You leave them alone!"

"No need to be aggressive, Paul. I promise you that I'll not be any trouble to either of them, whatever happens. You have my word."

"Then let's just get on with it, Simon. You're calling the shots, as usual. I'd really like to get this over with. Where to, Simon? Where are we going?"

"We're going to town. Do you want me to drive?"

"Just give me directions," Paul said. "Remember what happened last time I let you drive the car!"

Simon laughed. "You know, Paul, I really do like you - and I admire you for the way you've taken all of this. I do hope that this works out for both of us. Somewhere out there is a body just waiting for me to jump in. All I need is the little secret of how to get that "ticker" going - how to get the life force flowing again. We can both be winners tonight!"

"Know what, Simon? You're madder than me! There's no way back for you. Just accept it – you're dead! Nothing that happens tonight is going to change that."

"Now you're upsetting me. Don't be so negative. I have every faith in you securing a future for both of us."

"More likely we'll be having a drink at The Chair. And if we are, stay well away from me!"

Simon's tone changed. For the first time ever, Paul noticed an air of annoyance in his voice. "I think we should go now. Take the next left and drive us to the town centre. You know the multi-story car park on Bell Street? Turn in there and go right up to the top level."

"You're the boss!" Paul replied, feeling quite pleased that he had finally been able to ruffle Simon's feathers. "Cheer up! The Chair's not a bad pub!" he added, trying to force home his new advantage.

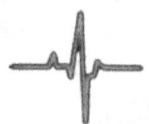

Chapter 43

As the Ford turned into the multi-story car park, Paul saw that the ticket barriers were already raised so that they could drive straight in without stopping. Paul wasn't sure if this was Simon's doing or if the barriers were always up at this time of night. He didn't bother to ask – it really didn't matter.

They followed the narrow spiral pathway to the rooftop level.

"Over there!" Simon pointed to the Bell Street side of the parking area.

The area was empty of other vehicles – just a vast expanse of tarmac with dozens of parking slots neatly marked in white and yellow paint.

Paul chose a slot about half way along the Bell Street wall and switched off the engine.

Behind them, the Jaguar appeared. Mitch chose a space in the central aisle about twenty yards from the Ford. He left the engine running but switched off the lights and applied the handbrake.

"Too close!" Simon said to Paul. The smile had returned to his face along with a wicked glint in his eyes. "Watch this!"

Paul turned in his seat and watched through the rear window of his car. Without any warning, the Jaguar screeched in reverse towards the far side of the car park, tyres smoking. It stopped, inches from the wall, perfectly parked between the white lines. Paul could see the surprise and terror on Robin and Mitch's faces.

"That's better!" Simon laughed.

Inside the Jaguar, the two men looked at each other, neither quite believing what had just happened.

"No one pisses about with me like this!" Mitch suddenly raged, grabbing for the door handle of the Jag.

As he did so, there was a distinct click as the doors of the Jaguar locked. Mitch tried the unlock lever. Nothing happened. Robin didn't even bother to try the passenger door. As they looked at each other again, two mobile phones rang. Both men reached into their pockets. Both men watched as the screens of their mobiles clouded and then took on the scorched look both men had seen before. Their phones were useless.

"I guess that's just the point," Robin said. "It *is* a 'no-one' that's pissing with us. We're helpless, Mitch."

Simon turned away from the scene in the Jaguar and faced the front of the Ford again.

"Being dead does have its compensations. You can do all sorts of amazing stuff. It's great for pranks, except you never get the credit for them. All the same, it gets boring after a while."

"There's only one thing worse than a ghost," Paul said, looking at the grinning face, "and that's a crazy ghost! How in God's name did I get stuck with you?"

"It was that little nudge that you gave me on the M6, Paul. Just think, if you'd played fair that night, none of this would have happened. Cheats never prosper, that's what my old mum used to tell me."

"Bollocks!" Paul said, "You're just a bad loser and a piss-poor driver as well. I didn't nudge you - you just bottled it!"

"Sticks and stones," Simon replied. "Anyhow, it matters little. Here we are, Paul, and we've got things to do. You ready?"

"Whenever you say."

Simon got out of the Ford and walked round to Paul's door. Paul was already getting out.

"Follow me!" Simon said, as he walked towards a small grey service door that was next to the main pedestrian exit to the lifts. Paul followed him through the door and out of sight of Mitch and Robin.

From the Jaguar, Mitch and Robin watched as Paul reappeared on the far side of the safety barriers. He seemed to be walking on thin air. They could see that he was talking.

"Oh no! Dear God, no!" Mitch whispered. He tore at the door handle again.

Robin placed a calming hand on his arm. "We're just observers in all this. There's nothing we can do!" he said.

"A leap of faith – a step into the unknown!" Simon crowed, looking straight into Paul's eyes. Can you really do it?"

"Do I have a choice?"

"Oh yes, Paul! You have a choice. This has to be of your own free will. Last time, in the car, I gave you no choice. I was impetuous. This time *you* have to choose to die. You see, I don't believe you'd be crazy enough to jump if you didn't know that you could survive. I have to find out if you have that secret, Paul. You do understand, don't you?"

"So if I choose not to jump, you'll know that there is no secret, no magic formula of survival. If that's the case, you might as well leave me in peace."

"I think that I would need to see you die before I could ever know that for certain, Paul. You don't have to jump, but you know how the game goes, if you choose not to do it now, I'll be everywhere in your life until you're ready to change your mind."

Resignedly, Paul climbed onto the low wall that surrounded the service pathway around the car park. He didn't look down into the blackness. Instead, on unsteady legs, he turned and faced inwards toward the parked Jaguar. He could see the looks of terror and disbelief on his father and his friend's faces.

Paul raised both his arms to shoulder level, making his body into the shape of a cross.

"Goodbye, Simon! May you rot in Hell!"

Slowly, he fell backwards into the night.

"No!" Mitch screamed, as he watched his only son disappear.

The locks on the Jaguar doors clicked. Mitch and Robin ran from the car, across the car park to the point where they had seen Paul fall. It was impossible to see past the service pathway Paul had fallen from. They ran for the grey door that Simon and Paul had used. It was locked.

Without a word, they ran back to the Jag. Mitch smoked the tyres towards the exit, round and round down the spiral ramp, bouncing the car off the concrete walls.

As they reached the ground level, Mitch realised that the exit would not take them out onto Bell Street, where Paul had fallen. Ignoring the "No Exit" signs, he headed for the entrance they had used. The ticket barriers were down. Mitch didn't care. The Jaguar smashed through the obstacle. The windscreen remained in tact.

They were out onto Bell Street.

Mitch turned the headlights to full beam. The street seemed empty. He edged the car forwards, at low speed, dreading what he might see. About fifty yards from the entrance, a shape lay in the gutter.

He stopped the car twenty yards short of the shape. The two men stared through the windscreen.

Mitch opened his door to get out. He looked back at Robin.

"I'm sorry! I can't!" Robin said.

Robin watched in horror as Mitch approached what had to be the smashed body of his son. About five yards short of the shape, Mitch sank to his knees, his hands covering his face. Robin threw the door of the Jaguar open, and vomited.

By the time he looked up, Mitch was walking slowly back towards the car. His expression was blank.

"It's not him!" Mitch said, his voice shaking. "It's just an old cardboard carton that somebody's dumped. It's not Paul. He's not here. I can see right to the end of the building. There's nothing. What the hell is going on? Where's my son, Robin? Where's Paul?"

They looked upwards into the night sky wondering if there was anywhere that a falling body could have become stuck before reaching the ground. The walls of the car park were sheer. If Paul had jumped, he must be here.

"He's alive!" Robin said. "He was right. Simon couldn't kill him. It's all part of the game. He's alive, Mitch. He must still be alive."

"Then where in God's name is he?" Mitch begged.

"Come on," Robin said excitedly, "We have to go back to his car."

—⎠⎮⎝—

When they reached the roof level of the car park, the Ford was gone.

"He must be looking for us," Robin said. "What do we do? Wait here or head home?"

After several minutes of waiting and shouting his name, Mitch and Robin decided that home was the best option.

"He's probably waiting for us!" Robin said hopefully. "Christ! How stupid! Call his mobile. Why haven't we called his mobile?"

Robin reached for his phone, which was, of course, functional again. He found Paul's number in his directory and pressed call.

"Number not recognised" came up.

"Shit!" Robin exclaimed, and tried again. "You try, Mitch, maybe my phone's knackered."

Mitch tried, but had the same result.

"Let's just get home."

When they reached Paul's house, no car was in the drive.

"What now?" Robin asked.

"I guess we just wait!"

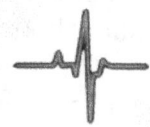

Chapter 44

As Paul fell slowly backwards, his feeling of mind-numbing fear evaporated and was instantly replaced by a sense of elation – of absolute freedom.

Falling...falling...falling, just like in a dream.

Soon the ground would rush up and devour him. He cared not!

Falling through space...through time...through emptiness ...falling, falling.

Not falling – flying. He was flying. He could fly!

He turned his body to face the ground below. Just blackness.

He turned on his back again facing the stars. There was no wind, not a breath of air. He was in a vacuum, floating, gliding.

"Look at me, you stupid dead person!" he shouted. "How do you like this, you bastard? You're dead and I'm flying. Go to hell! I'm still alive!"

He focussed on one particular star that shone brighter than all the rest. It seemed to be getting nearer and nearer, dropping from the night sky.

A concentrated beam of light was piercing his left eye - now moving to his right eye and back to the left again.

It was then that he heard the voice!

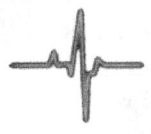

Chapter 45

"Paul? Can you hear me Paul? Are you awake? Paul, you can open your eyes now."

Paul tried to focus his mind. He could feel that his outstretched arms were being gently held. His vision was blurred. He could make out the end of the pen-like torch that was being shone into his eyes but beyond that, nothing was clear.

He tried to speak, but his throat felt dry and sore.

"Don't worry, Paul," the voice said. "You're very safe. Just take your time. There's no hurry. Can you squeeze my hand, Paul?

The man's voice kept talking in calm, low tones.

Paul continued to try to focus. This was all very strange. He tried to remember, but his memory was a blank.

He felt a cold, wet flannel pressed gently against his lips. He tried to suck the moisture to sooth his burning throat.

"Well done, Paul," the voice said. "I'll be here with you, don't worry. Try to relax. You've just had a very long sleep, and waking up is bound to be difficult."

Paul considered the new piece of information: "a very long sleep." What was that all about? He went to his memory again for help, but no help came.

"Where am I?" he tried to croak.

"That's fantastic, Paul," the voice said, obviously quite excited. "Paul, we're going to put a straw in your mouth so that you can drink. It's only water. Take a sip if you can. Just a sip!"

Paul felt the straw on his lips. The cool liquid felt good in his mouth. He choked as he tried to swallow. The straw was quickly removed. After a moment he felt it again and this time was able to get some of the water down.

"Where am I?" He asked again, this time more strongly.

"You're in a nursing home, Paul. I'm Doctor Rossi. You're in very safe hands, Paul. You have nothing to worry about. Everything is going to be fine."

"How?" Paul asked.

"Listen, Paul, I'm going to ask you a couple of simple questions. What's your mother's name, Paul?"

"Grace," Paul managed.

"And your father?"

"Mitch – Mitchell Ford. Why do you ask? Can I have more water?"

He felt the straw back on his lips. This time he drank a little more.

"I'm trying to find out how much you remember, Paul. Will you try to help me?"

"Ask away," Paul croaked. "Before you ask, my wife's name is Jo, Where is Jo? Is she here?"

"We're getting her here right now, Paul, and your mother and father. Why don't you try to relax for a while? No more questions from me just now. Emma will stay with you. Emma is your nurse. She'll give you more water if you want it. It's best if you don't try to talk too much. I'll be back in a little while. Welcome back, Paul."

Paul didn't quite understand the last comment. "Welcome back?" What did that mean?

"More water, please."

The straw was returned to his lips.

He felt a soft hand on his forehead. His eyes still wouldn't focus properly but he could make out the form of a person standing over him – a woman. She smelt so good.

"Emma, what's happened to me?"

"I think you'd be better do as Dr Rossi suggested," Emma replied. "Just relax, Paul. You've taken a massive step forwards today. Best to take your time and to not try to go too far too quickly. The doctor will talk to you again soon. I'd better not go telling you things that he wants to tell you himself, had I?"

"Can I see Jo, and my parents?"

"All in good time, Paul. I'm sure they'll be here soon."

Paul decided that Emma had a sexy voice. At least he was beginning to think more clearly. He only wished that he could see her clearly. He took another drink and then closed his still-blurry eyes – not to sleep, just to think.

It took many days, and many hours of talking with doctors and nurses and family, before Paul began to fully understand that almost a year of his life had been lost in "sleep."

His recovery stunned the doctors who had attended him. Paul became something of a celebrity, receiving visits from the team that had cared for him in Wolverhampton's Royal Hospital as well as from specialists at various other hospitals who studied and treated mental disorders.

It wasn't just the speed of recovery that was amazing. The simple fact that Paul appeared to have come through his year of coma without any adverse effect was remarkable – almost unbelievable.

His medical team held many discussions, sometimes with Jo and Paul's parents, during which they decided what Paul should be told and what should be kept from him.

His long-term memory was perfect. He could go back with ease to school days, college, drama school and his early acting career. He could remember huge passages of dialogue that he had learned for plays he had performed in. Everything was clear in his mind, right up to his audition for *The Chair* and the start of his journey home from Glasgow.

It was at this point that his memory started to fail. There were certain things that he did remember vividly: the pub, his visit to his father's golf club, and Martin, the hypnotist. He remembered Jo's friend Sally and that Robin had come and stayed with him for a few days (although he couldn't remember why.). But there was no mention of his demon. Simon had gone.

Paul was told that The Chair, the visit to the golf club, and Martin the hypnotist, were all part of an intricate dream and soon he was able to accept that many of his most recent memories were simply a part of that dream.

Throughout his mental rehabilitation, there was always the worry that unwanted memories would be stirred and he was encouraged not to dwell on any recent memory. Information about the accident, including the fatality, was left untouched. He was given no detail of his dramatic return to consciousness, about the flailing arms and the shouts of "You're dead" and "I'm still alive!" The simple truth was that he had been involved in an horrific accident and that he had been treated for a while in The Royal Hospital in Wolverhampton. When it became obvious that his condition was basically untreatable and that only time would decide his fate, his father had insisted he should be moved to The Beeches Nursing Home near Shrewsbury, close to Paul's parents' house. For many months, Doctor Rossi and his staff had cared for him. Everything else since his journey home from Glasgow was fantasy.

Gradually, Paul was happy to accept the truth. He was happy to be alive.

Apart from his mental rehab, his physical rehabilitation was long and arduous. Hour after hour of physiotherapy was necessary to coax wasted muscle back to full working order.

After a full month, Paul was nearing the time that he could return to a normal life. His stay at The Beeches had given him ample time to realise the massive impact that his accident had on his wife and his parents - how their lives had been thrown into turmoil whilst he had been sleeping.

When the day of leaving finally arrived, emotions were running high. Though everyone at The Beeches was thrilled that

Paul should be going home fully recovered, they were all sorry to be losing their "star" patient.

Paul promised to return to see them often and thanked them for giving him his life back.

Jo drove them home, the two of them close to tears for most of the way.

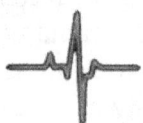

Chapter 46

It's surprising how quickly life can return to normal following extreme circumstances. The human mind seems to have a way of coping. Not necessarily forgetting – but at least dealing with situations that challenge life itself. When you consider natural disasters – tsunamis, earthquakes, volcanic eruptions – and see how soon the rebuilding of shattered lives begins, you realise that, between our ears, we have a pretty tough piece of kit.

In the weeks and months that followed his return home with Jo, Paul's life soon became much the same as he had left it.

He spent a while just catching up with things. Much had gone on during his year "away."

The Euro had fallen into crisis. There had been a highly successful home Olympic Games. The price of petrol had rocketed. His beloved Wolverhampton Wanderers had been relegated. There were the usual "hot spots" of political and civilian unrest around the world. Dictators had been deposed and new regimes had been born. There were notable births, deaths and marriages to catch up on.

Jo had religiously kept every Sunday newspaper for him. She had never lost faith that he would come back one day. Paul spent many hours trying, in some way, to relive the year that he had lost.

He even went to play golf with his father. The golf club proved to be very different from the place he remembered in his dreams. The clubhouse was a just a small, modern redbrick building that housed a bar and a pro shop. There was no Mrs B with her mountains of bacon rolls. The car park was full of family saloons. Mitch's Jaguar was the "stand-out" vehicle. At the end of the round, Paul still hated golf but he treasured the time spent with his Dad.

Paul and Jo found that their marriage and their friendship were stronger than ever. They were seldom apart for long. Both knew that they had been given a second chance and both were determined to grab the opportunity with both hands. They were blissfully happy.

Jo continued to teach and Paul began resurrecting his acting career, with the help of his good friend Robin. Life was good!

It was Saturday afternoon. Jo had been to the hairdresser's and to the supermarket. Paul had stayed in to watch the sport on television. He had gone to the kitchen and was making coffee when he heard the front door open.

"Hi honey! I'm home."

"Hi, Jo, I'm just boiling the kettle. Do you want a cup?"

"Yes, please!" came the reply, "I'm just getting the last bags out of the car."

Paul made two mugs of coffee and waited for Jo to return.

When Jo came back, she went into the living room with a new table lamp that she had bought.

"I met an old friend of yours at the supermarket." she shouted, "Nice guy. He seemed to know me, but I can't remember meeting him before. He said he'd pop in and see you soon. Said his name was Simon!"

Jo heard the coffee mug smash on the kitchen floor.

"Paul? Paul, are you okay?"

When Jo reached the kitchen, Paul was on his knees. His shirt was soaked with coffee. The mug lay smashed all around him. His expression was blank. He was staring straight ahead through dead eyes. His mouth hung open.

Jo rushed to kneel beside him.

"Paul! What is it? Say something, Paul. You look like you've seen a ghost!"

Paul is being cared for in a private home for the mentally ill.

He lives in a dream world. He has a friend called Simon who visits him most days. They chat about life and death and racing. They talk a lot about a pub they both know called The Chair. Simon can do tricks. Paul can fly. Simon's a dreadful driver. Paul knows a very special secret – but he'll never tell!

No one else can see Simon. Paul won't talk to anyone, except his friend.

This may be "The End" - but you can never be sure!

Author's note

The story that I set out to write is very different from the story that you have just read.

Having completed *The Chair*, I sat and stared at my computer screen. This is not my book. These are not my thoughts. I have been the typist, not the author! That's how it felt.

The story of *The Chair* just happened! It wasn't planned. I never knew what the next page was going say. It was as if I was reading the book, not writing it.

Now that it's done, I have very mixed feelings. I think that *The Chair* is a good story. I hope that *The Chair* is nothing more than a good story.

Writing this account has created doubts in my mind – doubts that I never wanted or needed. It has taken me to places that I would rather not have visited. It has made me challenge all that I believe to be real.

Maybe death is the only reality.
We will only know when we walk through the front door of
THE CHAIR.

About the Author

Eric Pullin was born in Wolverhampton, England in 1946.

He started his working life as a primary school teacher. Later, he joined Goodyear Racing Division which led to his love of Formula 1 motor racing and rallying. He was also a member of the European Goodyear Airship crew.

On the birth of his first grand daughter, Eric decided to write a children's bedtime story as a special gift. Though he had never written before, once he began writing, about his cat called Digweed, he found that he could not stop and instead of producing a short bedtime story, he ended up with a full length novel called "Digweed the Cat".

The book sat on a shelf for 7 years until Lucy was old enough to read the story for herself but now she loves her Grampy's gift.

The birth of his second grand daughter Lulah, two years later, started him writing again and this time he produced a short bedtime tale called "Why Animals Don't Talk". This story, written in verse, proved so popular, that Eric decided to write more "Why" stories and soon he had written "Why Owls are The Wisest Birds", "Why There Are Waves On The Sea", "Why Stars Come Out At Night", and many more stories and so "The Why Series" was born.

This success made it possible for him to work in schools helping children with their creative writing and once again, Eric found himself at the front of classrooms all over the U.K. The one time teacher had seen his life go full circle and he is thrilled to be working with children once again.

In 2012 an Italian author friend, Annarita Guarnieri, suggested that he submit his first book "Digweed the Cat" to her publishers - Inknbeans Press.

His family will tell you that he's just an "old softee". Eric wouldn't want things to be any other way.

If you've enjoyed Digweed's adventures, or if you have comments or constructive criticism, you can reach Eric Pullin at Pullin@inknbeans.com

Eric's books, are available at fine booksellers everywhere and at Inknbeans Press.

Look for these other fine authors from Inknbeans Press:

Enjae Edwards, *You'll Wake Up One Morning*
Susan Wells Bennett, *The Brass Monkey Series*
Jim Burkett, *The Nick West Series*
Rusty Coats, *Out of Touch*
Kitty Sutton, *Mysteries From the Trail of Tears*
Dea Lenihan, *Out of This World Series*
Dawn Hood, *God's Pinky Promises*
David Rowinski, *The Open Pillow*
Dorothy Legge, *Poems of Faith and Love*
Ey Wade, *In My Sister's World*
Perle Butcher Lyon, *The Dutch Doctor*
Annarita Guarnieri, *The Importance of Being Shine*
Hugh Ashton, *The Deed Box of John H Watson, MD*
Nickie Storey, *The Grimsley Hollow Series*
Jt Sather, *How to Survive When the Bottom Drops Out*
Virginia Czaja, *Get Real*
Jackie Williams, *the Tori-Jean, No! series*
Liam McCaughey, *Collected Werks*
Jt Sather, *How to Survive When the Bottom Drops Out*

Fresh Books Brewed Daily

www.ingramcontent.com/pod-product-compliance
Lightning Source LLC
Chambersburg PA
CBHW070822120626
46556CB00002B/620